# TALES
*from the*
# ETERNAL CAFÉ

## stories by
## JANET HAMILL

THREE ROOMS PRESS
NEW YORK

Also by Janet Hamill
*Body of Water*
*Lost Ceilings*
*Nostalgia of the Infinite*
*The Temple*
*Troublante*

Some of these tales previously appeared in *BOMB Magazine*,
*Oyez Review*, and the anthologies *Up Late: American Poetry
Since 1970* (4 Walls 8 Windows), *Living with the Animals*
(Faber and Faber), and *Have a NYC: New York Short Stories*
(Three Rooms Press).

*Tales from the Eternal Café*
stories by Janet Hamill

Copyright ©2014 by Janet Hamill

All rights reserved. No part of this book may be reproduced in any form or by
any electronic or mechanical means, including information storage and retrieval
systems, without permission in writing from the publisher, except by a reviewer,
who may quote brief passages in a review. For permissions, please write to address
below or email editor@threeroomspress.com. Any members of education institutions
wishing to photocopy or electronically reproduce part or all of the work for classroom
use, or publishers who would like to obtain permission to include the work in an
anthology, should send their inquiries to Three Rooms Press,
51 MacDougal Street, #290, New York, NY 10012.

First Edition

ISBN: 978-0-9895125-0-3
Library of Congress Control Number: 2013947728

Author photo:
Bryan Hamill

Cover and interior design:
KG Design International (katgeorges.com)

Published by Three Rooms Press, New York, NY
threeroomspress.com | facebook.com/threeroomspress

*to Joe*

# CONTENTS

*Introduction*. . . . . . . . . . . . . . . . . . . . . . . . . . . . . . . . . . . . . . . i

Baudelaire at the Prince of Wales . . . . . . . . . . . . . . . . . . . . . . 1

Two Women and a White Umbrella. . . . . . . . . . . . . . . . . . 14

The Serenity of the Scholar . . . . . . . . . . . . . . . . . . . . . . . . . .25

Espresso Cinecittà. . . . . . . . . . . . . . . . . . . . . . . . . . . . . . . . . .28

Ursula and the Sublime . . . . . . . . . . . . . . . . . . . . . . . . . . . . .59

Blue Corpus Christi . . . . . . . . . . . . . . . . . . . . . . . . . . . . . . . .73

Tangiers Dejoun. . . . . . . . . . . . . . . . . . . . . . . . . . . . . . . . . . .89

Novalis . . . . . . . . . . . . . . . . . . . . . . . . . . . . . . . . . . . . . . . . .108

Patio of the Orange Trees. . . . . . . . . . . . . . . . . . . . . . . . . . .120

The Birds of the Air . . . . . . . . . . . . . . . . . . . . . . . . . . . . . . .124

The White Lion . . . . . . . . . . . . . . . . . . . . . . . . . . . . . . . . . .129

The Passage of Juana Inez. . . . . . . . . . . . . . . . . . . . . . . . . . .132

Autumn Melancholy. . . . . . . . . . . . . . . . . . . . . . . . . . . . . . .139

Fire Worshippers. . . . . . . . . . . . . . . . . . . . . . . . . . . . . . . . . .143

The Astronomer . . . . . . . . . . . . . . . . . . . . . . . . . . . . . . . . . .147

Pictures at an Exhibition . . . . . . . . . . . . . . . . . . . . . . . . . . . 151

Lake of the Buddhas. . . . . . . . . . . . . . . . . . . . . . . . . . . . . . .158

Time is the substance I am made of. Time is a river which sweeps me along, but I am the river; it is a tiger which destroys me, but I am the tiger; it is a fire which consumes me, but I am the fire.

—Jorge Luis Borges, *Labyrinths*

# *Introduction*

IN THE WORLD OF LITERATURE, THE café has long served as a
sanctuary for its conception as well as an escape from its
blessed tyranny. In the tales offered here, one may picture the
melancholic cafés of the nineteenth century, where the poet,
drowned in obscurity, pens his masterpiece and downs his
absinthe. It is impossible to ignore the music wafting from an
Italian modernist café hosting a parade of elegant savages who
form the stylishly depraved sweet life, or feel the unease that
permeates a Moroccan café where the pungent fragrance of
mint tea and hashish can cloud and vibrate the senses.

This is the realm of The Eternal Café—at once existent and
envisioned—given visceral substance by the poet Janet Hamill.
The tales birthed in this glowing sphere speak not only of her
expansive visionary power and well-traveled life but of her
devotion to copious research. Her work ranges from cinematic
tales that are fresh and present to those written in the tradition
of storytellers throughout time. Her tales told within cafés
conjure up the atmosphere of a plethora of eras, laying out

mysteries both decadent and divine. We notice a different light falling on the complex movements of her characters, separate skies, separate stars.

Janet and I befriended as we were college girls in rural South Jersey, where there were no cafés to serve our dreams or expectations. Thus we were obliged to construct our own, composited by the stones of our mutual imagination. Cafés worthy of the poets and artists we adored, paying homage to their lively gossip and dissertation. Our projected selves, relaxed within the arcane walls of our phantom cafés and dressed in the fabrics of whatever era we fixated on, discoursed with Surrealists in Paris, Romantic poets in the Lake District, and the Beats in Tangiers. Armed with the memory of these redoubtable experiences, we each set out on our own.

Janet went on to travel, from Juárez to Rome to Marrakesh, and frequented such cafés herself. After years of contemplation and study she created The Eternal Café—a meeting place well worthy of the muse, melding universes and serving up elixirs unimaginable.

There is nothing more wonderful than the café, and the tales that are drawn from them. Long live the café—whether found on the dark backstreet, the fashionable thoroughfare, or the pages of a book! Within them, as through these tales, we gain entrance to the history of a world where madams rub shoulders with mystics and visionaries with vagabonds.

*—Patti Smith*

# TALES
*from the*
# ETERNAL
# CAFÉ

# Baudelaire at the Prince of Wales

ALLOW ME TO INTRODUCE MYSELF. I'M a debtor, pornographer, and unreformed Socialist. I have a gift for conversation and an amusing take on everything, including my self-imposed exile in Belgium. I am Coco Poulet Malassis, who despite my ignoble achievements and reputation as a loyal, faithful friend, will be remembered solely as the publisher of Charles Baudelaire's first collection. (Well, perhaps with this new invention of photography, my most distinguished features— my goatee and embroidered skull cap—will be remembered.)

Charles and I first met in the heady days of '47–'48, the days of the first communard, when everyone was setting up barricades and calling for a Republic. Our politics were compatible, and we hated anything that spoke of convention.

Our temperaments were, and are, very different. Charles is inclined to the serious and spiritual, while I laugh at everything.

At the time of our first meeting, Charles was already gaining a reputation for his poetry. Aside from its originality and craft, it was said to be filled with debauchery. Of course, that appealed to me. Anything to shock the bourgeoisie. He was looking for a publisher, and while I wasn't a publisher per se, I came from a long line of printers. I undertook the production of Charles's first book, and our friendship was sealed.

Now in our forties, Charles and I both live in Brussels—Charles, as is his fashion, at the Hôtel du Grand Miroir, I in more humble quarters. Charles sees his exile as something temporary, the result of insurmountable debts in Paris, which he came here hoping to annihilate. My stay will likely be of a more permanent nature, my debt and politics so egregious to the French that I'd be thrown into prison should I return. I rather like it here and don't care if I ever see Paris again. I get by publishing pornography and anti-Second Empire tracts, which I arrange to have smuggled across the border into France. Charles, on the other hand, despises Brussels and all things Belgian. He gets by with what remains of his dwindling inheritance.

I'd been in Brussels for several years when Charles arrived in '64. He came with high hopes, put in his head by Belgian art dealer Arthur Stevens—high hopes of giving lectures and finding a new publisher. The former resulted in several disasters, the latter never materialized. He was already suffering from the tertiary stages of syphilis when he arrived, and I'd seen a rapid decline in his health during his stay. Even so, we make a habit of meeting at our favorite café, the Prince of Wales, conveniently located across the Place de Musée from the main post office. Originally established in 1815 by a veteran of the battle of Waterloo, it's one of a handful of English-style pubs or taverns in Brussels patronized by Frenchmen fleeing the intolerable politics at home. Along with the French, the café attracts their Belgian and British sympathizers. Artists and writers for the most part, they enjoy the anti-Napoleon III bias of the café's newspapers and the British ales, considered far superior to syrupy Flemish *faros*.

ONE LATE AFTERNOON, I WAS SEATED in the back room when Charles came in. Like me, he avoided the crowded outer room with its gentleman's-club atmosphere and headed straight for the back room. I hadn't seen him in almost two weeks, and I was stunned by his appearance. Usually impeccable, his clothes were uncharacteristically disheveled, he had a few days growth on his normally smooth face, and his hair was unwashed and hung in long locks over his shoulders. His cheeks were ashen, his eyes sunken and shadowed. My first thought was that he'd been drinking excessively, a nasty habit he'd developed in exile.

He sat across from me in a quiet corner. He didn't greet me. I wasn't certain he even knew who I was. I watched him remove his Inverness cape, his black wide-brimmed hat, and the seda-tive-soaked turban he wore beneath it to relieve his migraines. He laid them on the chair beside him and glanced around the room, looking for what I don't know.

He sat silently staring into space then finally spoke in a barely audible voice. He said he felt as though he was twenty years old, sitting in his cabin on the Paquebot-des-Mers-du-Sud. In his mind, the room's compactness, its low ceiling, wood paneling, and low hanging lamp over the table must have simulated his cabin when he was bound for Calcutta under the orders of his stepfather, General Aupick, who thought an ocean voyage would cure him of poetry.

He said he felt dizzy. He didn't know if it was vertigo or if he was seasick. He said water must be flooding the hold, giving the ship a list to starboard. He gripped the bottom of his chair to steady himself. He said we were closeted in a tight cabin, just north of the Tropic of Capricorn, to the east of Madagascar. We were two days away from the Maldives, sailing turbulent waters, with a kerosene lamp overhead, swinging back and forth.

He started to concentrate on a faint patch of light pouring through the room's single window. He said the light danced on the floor planks, creating patterns of a mast, a sail, and rigging. The dancing patch became a blazing orb, high in a vermilion sky. He suggested we surrender to the rough rhythm of the sea. We were sailing toward ornate mansions dotting the shore of a remote island.

As I said, I'd been observing a definite decline in Charles's condition since his arrival in Brussels, but his words on this occasion were more disquieting than ever. I was accustomed to his complaints of migraines, stiffness, losing his balance, and increasing number of seizures. I knew his temperament was getting more and more unpredictable and he was drinking more. I saw his growing agitation, confusion, and forgetfulness, his tendency to keep to himself or fail to show for engagements. I was aware of his prolonged episodes of despondency, but never before had I known him to be as abstracted from his surroundings as he was at that moment.

He sat silently. Then I spoke. "My dear Charles, your remote island is the Prince of Wales."

Charles's eyes stayed fixed on the distance, staring at his shoreline.

"Charles, look, it's me, Coco!"

"Captain Saliz," he said, addressing me as the captain of the Paquebot-des-Mers-du-Sud, "I find the rough seas no longer disturb me. Soon it will be evening, and the stucco villas on the coast will pick up the glow of the moon."

To me, Charles's delusion was an alarming indication that his disease had reached his brain. Syphilis often manifested as dementia in its end stage. My concern prompted me to signal for service in the hope that food and drink would bring him to his senses.

"Good evening, gentlemen. What can I bring you?" The waitress at the Prince of Wales was a dark-haired, bronze-skinned beauty named Marie. She could easily have passed for a young Jeanne Duval, Charles's Creole mistress. Her exotic looks came from a strain of East Indian blood mixed with her native Dutch. She was the wife of Harry Turner, the café proprietor.

I ordered ale and steak tartar with porter and egg, a specialty of the house.

"And Monsieur Baudelaire . . . ?"

Baudelaire looked adoringly at Marie and took her hand. "Madame de Bragard," he said, "should you ever leave Mauritius and visit us in France, you will not be without admirers."

I saw the confusion in Marie's face. "Don't mind him. He's reenacting an old sea voyage."

"Will Madame be serving brandy after dinner?" Charles inquired.

Marie withdrew her hand and looked to me for direction.

"Monsieur Baudelaire would like a brandy."

Marie nodded, smiled sympathetically, and went to fetch the order.

Charles followed her graceful movements as she disappeared into the large room, taking his voyage vision with her. He snapped out of his trance and finally looked across, opaque glaze gone from his eyes.

"Coco! How good to see you," he said, making the transition from ocean vessel to the Prince of Wales with ease. "I'm glad you chose the small room. The main room is crowded with louts, noisy revolutionaries still wearing the red cravats of their youth. It's so tiresome."

"I'm worried about you, Charles. I haven't seen you in over a week, and you just addressed me as Captain Saliz and Marie as Madame de Bragard?"

"The Paquebot-des-Mers-du-Sud! And Madame de Bragard, the wife of the Maldivian plantation owner. I met her on my aborted trip to India."

"One and the same, *une dame Creole*?"

"The same. I hope I didn't embarrass her. I wanted to order a brandy."

"I've ordered one for you."

Baudelaire reached into his pocket and withdrew two letters. "After ten days, ten days, this is all that was waiting for me at the post office! As if that weren't enough of a disappointment, they weren't sufficiently franked. I had to pay to have them released."

"Who do you hear from?"

"My mother and a creditor."

"Just one creditor? You're lucky, Charles! I received six letters from six different creditors today."

Baudelaire opened his mother's letter and tried to read it. "I can't understand this. The words make no sense. Maybe it's my eyes. Would you mind reading it for me?"

I took the letter and read aloud: *My Dearest, Is it possible that you exaggerate the gravity of your illness? I took the liberty of reading your complaints to Dr. Porché here in Honfleur. He thinks you may be suffering from nervous exhaustion. In which case, he says you don't need more medicine. It's best you take long walks and cold baths. . . .*

Charles interrupted my reading. "Long walks and cold baths! Can my mother actually think they would put an end to my migraines? She's become so indoctrinated by this quack, Porché. She's taking his word over mine. To suggest that I don't need medication! Without laudanum and quinine I wouldn't be alive!"

I reacted calmly. "Charles, she doesn't even know the true nature of your illness. Shall I continue?"

"No." Baudelaire picked up his turban and wrapped it around his temples. "Her letter's only brought back my head pain. The thought of writing to her and telling her about the agonies I've endured would be worse than the agonies I've endured. God, it was horrific! Cold sweats, cramping, vomiting. Head pains like nails piercing my skull. I couldn't stand without losing my balance. Once I pulled down all of the curtains from the window and knocked over my desk. Worse of all, I couldn't sleep. The ceiling stains, transforming into faces. . . ."

"What faces . . . ?"

"All the faces that I'll never see again. My face, the one painted by Emile Deroy when I lived on the Île de la Cité, the face of the young flâneur. I was so confident then, before I squandered the bulk of my inheritance on kid gloves, Moroccan bindings, the best Bordeaux and hashish. The shape-shifting faces mocked me. I saw Jeanne's face in its copper radiance, her face with its voluptuous features sitting beside me in an open carriage in the Bois de Boulogne raising everyone's eyebrows. The dandy and his black Venus. Oh how she aroused my mind and my senses. And lastly, there was my mother's face in the days shortly after my father's death. I thought I finally had her to myself. She'd sit on the floor with me with her great, wide skirts, as I traced my future voyages on my maps. Of course, all that was before she married General Aupik."

"I'm sorry." I returned the letter to its envelope. "So, when did you last hear from Lemer?" I asked, referring to Baudelaire's agent in Paris.

"Weeks, weeks and weeks! The incompetent ass! He's yet to interest anyone in *Paradis artificial, Spleen de Paris,* or *Pauvre Belgique!* He's yet to get me payment for the latest volume of the Poe translations, nor has he convinced a single critic to review it. I was expecting letters from friends, checks. That's all I had to look forward to while I lie in my hotel room, haunted by those faces. I forced myself to blot out the faces and envision checks, enough checks to pay off my bills in Brussels and clear my debts back home. Then I could flee this sorry excuse for a country! After my visit to the post office, I feel forgotten."

"You've got to look on the bright side, Charles. You're developing a following among younger poets."

"Ah, yes, 'The School of Baudelaire.' Who are these poets? Verlaine and Mallarmé? Imitators! Ridiculous vampires! They suck my blood and spit it out in puerile facsimiles."

Marie returned with Baudelaire's brandy and my ale and steak tartare. She set them down and walked away without arousing so much as a glance from Charles.

"How can you eat that? I'd rather starve than ingest raw beef and egg."

"It's good for you; it tastes good, too. Helps thicken the blood."

"Well, the sight of it destroys any appetite I might have had. I doubt I'll eat decent food again until I'm seated once more at the Tour d'Argent. The Belgians wouldn't know good food if you put their noses in it. Fois gras in a pig's trough. *Pauvre Belgique!* What a brilliant title. You won't believe what I saw as I walked here."

"What did you see, Charles?"

"A funeral outside the Church of Sainte-Gudule. The haute bourgeoisie of Brussels mounting the steps. The lot of them, descendants of Breugel's peasants. You could strip the overfed merchants and their wives of their mourning clothes and find turnip-shaped gluttons underneath. The porcine bastards could fill the monstrance at the head of their procession with a thousand Congolese diamonds, and it wouldn't eradicate their base origins. I wished a downfall of frogs on them. I wanted the rain to turn into murrain. The casket open and slide through the gutter. Avaricious swine!"

"That's what you called the Parisians in the Bois when you were on your outings with Jeanne. Was Jeanne ever good for more than shocking, Charles?"

"Jeanne, my poor Jeanne. For all her bickering and cheating, our endless breakups and reunions, she was my muse. She's nearly blind now and suffering from paralysis. She's lost her teeth. She lives in a *maison de santé*. I write her and send what I can to pay expenses."

"I didn't know."

I ate and Baudelaire drank, sometimes mumbling incoherently, sometimes staring into space, shifting from the real to the imagined without discrimination or awareness.

I sought to anchor my friend in the here and now by directing his attention to Marie. She stood several tables away in the outer room, joking with a rowdy group.

Baudelaire mistook the waitress for Jeanne, surrounded by privileged brats outside the stage door after one of her burlesques. "I pledge, Malassis, to remove Mademoiselle Duval from this degrading station and house her in fine and fashionable quarters. I'll dress and bejewel her like a quadroon queen. Never again will she have to endure such leers."

"It's Marie Turner, Charles, not Jeanne. You're losing yourself again. Come! Let's play our game of reprobate and priest! I'll be the unregenerate atheist and you the Jesuit determined to save my soul from eternal damnation."

The suggestion focused Baudelaire's attention, and he pitched into the mock argument that never failed to entertain us.

As our game spiraled into elaborate debate, the Belgian photographer Neyt approached the table. Baudelaire was annoyed by the intrusion and ignored the photographer, but I was glad to see him. "Neyt . . . ," I said, gesturing to indicate an empty chair.

Neyt was especially pleased to see Charles. He'd photographed him two weeks earlier and carried a print from the sitting with him. He sat down and laid it on the table. Neyt had photographed Baudelaire on several occasions, and thought his latest effort to be the most impressive.

I was quick to agree. I liked the intelligence and look of noble defiance Neyt had captured, but Baudelaire regarded the image with disgust. He saw only unforgiving detail in his unkempt hair and coat and his loose cravat. He pushed the print away and blazed a look of fury at Neyt. "Do you enjoy documenting my decline? Where's my soul? Where's the fire in my eyes? You've gutted me and left me with a bleak, burnt gaze. Anyone who sees this will see a beaten man who can't afford a haircut. That's not a photograph of me. It's a photograph of my death mask!"

Neyt was speechless. I reiterated my admiration for the photograph and tried to assuage the poet's uncalled-for criticism.

Baudelaire pushed back his chair and stood up. He shot a glance into the large room, where Arthur Stevens and his bother Joseph, the painter, had just arrived. They were setting up a game of billiards. Charles headed toward them.

Neyt started after him, but I held him back. "Leave him be. He should be all right. If not, we're right here."

Neyt remained shaken by Baudelaire's response to his photographs. It wasn't just Charles's unexpected criticism that disturbed him. He had growing concerns for Baudelaire's health. He spoke to me about the dissolution and frailty he'd noticed in the past few months and the escalating incidents of erratic behavior. Neyt reinforced my fears that Charles's mind might have become invaded by his disease. He feared the time had come to place him in a *maison de santé*.

I told Neyt that Baudelaire, with his stubbornness and pride, would never enter a hospital of his own volition. Resolved to rescue the evening from gloom, I signaled to Marie to order ale for Neyt and another round for me and Charles.

While Neyt talked excitedly about the challenge photography was presenting to painting and the magical process of developing prints, I spotted what looked like trouble in the outer room. Joseph Stevens was quickly removing his waistcoat in front of a solemn, erect Baudelaire. Given Charles's mood, I was afraid Charles had offended the painter. I also knew that Charles was still angry with Arthur for having lured him to Belgium with empty promises. He hadn't forgiven him for the first lecture booked in a hayloft, his talk on Wagner drowned out by the bartering of merchants on the ground level. The humiliation still stung. Perhaps Joseph was interceding on Arthur's behalf after a volatile exchange.

Anticipating a brawl, I rose and started for the billiards table, but before I left the back room, I saw Joseph smile. He was handing his russet waistcoat to Charles and patting him on the shoulder. The two spoke briefly and shook hands. Then Baudelaire shook hands with Arthur and walked back to the table.

With his state improved, Baudelaire looked again at Neyt's photograph. "Still examining the coroner's document, eh? 'Portrait of the poet, dead, age forty-six.'" Charles put his hand on Neyt's forearm. "Joseph Stevens has made a gift to me of his waistcoat. I've praised it so many times; he says it's mine by right of admiration. I love its copper color, the color of the autumn."

"A sentimental color, Baudelaire?"

"Perhaps, Neyt. The color reminds me of certain vintage exotic women who, like the autumn sun, have lost their potency but still hold a fading fascination. All that Joseph has asked in return is that I write a piece in praise of the dogs of the poor. He makes a living painting the purebred, pampered pets of the rich, but his personal liking is for mutts. I like the idea. A piece on the dogs of the gutter for *Spleen de Paris*."

Charles picked up his glass and swallowed its contents in one gulp. When he put the glass down, his mind made another shift. He stared at the overhead lamp, once more swaying like a ship's lantern. Squarely, he addressed me. "We all belong to death, Captain Saliz. The beginning is the beginning of our ends. Such is the pull of death. Whether we dive into heaven or hell, we do it with our arms and eyes wide open. We're like sailors hearing the call of the Sirens, unable to resist the hypnotic pull!"

Baudelaire's eyes clouded. He shivered. "I feel cold and stiff. The palaces I see are made of ice, Captain. Soon we'll be entombed in snow."

I motioned to Madame Turner to bring another brandy. "Drink up, Charles."

Baudelaire put the waistcoat on under his jacket. "The fit is perfect! May this cloth protect me from the cold and warm me like the sun of October afternoons."

"More brandy will warm you, Charles."

"The lantern is hardly swaying now. The seas must be calming as we approach the island. Don't you think so, Captain?"

"Yes, Charles, the seas are calming," I said, looking anxiously at Neyt.

"Good! I'd like to go on deck and wait for the stars. The stars are at their brightest when it's cold. They sparkle like chips of crystal chandeliers."

Baudelaire threw his cape over his shoulders and put his hat over his turban. He reached into his pocket to pay for his brandies, but Neyt stopped him. "My pleasure," the photographer said. "Save your money and settle up at the hotel."

"Thank you. I don't believe we've met. Are you traveling all the way to India?"

Baudelaire looked around the crowded, smoky café, now thoroughly crowded in both rooms. I was certain that he had no idea where he actually was.

"Let me walk you back to the Grand Miroir, Charles. You need rest."

"Not rest, Captain, work! I'll write through the night in my cabin!"

"Please, I insist. You need a guiding hand."

"No, I have the dogs of the streets, the strays to which I must pay homage. They'll accompany me on deck."

"If you insist," I said. "I'll check in on you in the morning." There was no point in expressing my concerns. He wouldn't have understood them.

Baudelaire took a last look at Neyt's photograph and grinned. "The well isn't dry yet. It's just been replenished by our hostess's excellent brandy. Tonight its incandescent power will allow me to reach deep and draw buckets of glittering vowels and consonants. I'll write until the sun rises, lighting the way to polar palaces."

The poet drained his third brandy and walked unsteadily to the door of the Prince of Wales. With his mother's letter and the creditor's notice left behind on the café table, he stepped out into the damp night, well determined to keep his appointment with the sublime.

# Two Women and
# a White Umbrella

WHEN EDWARD DIED IN 1951, I had little interest in staying on
in Venice. I'd long lost interest in our tourist gallery, selling
reproductions of the Grand Canal—though Canaletto, Turner,
and Monet had allowed us to live well in our honeymoon city.
I was in my late fifties in '51, and at that age, without children
or any other reason to maintain a three-story house, I bought a
small apartment to keep a foothold in my adored, slowly
sinking paradise and moved to Feltre, a two-hour drive north
of Venice by train.

Life is quiet in this town, nestled in the foothills of the
Italian Alps. My large apartment, the entire top floor of a grand
old house, is more than sufficient. The local people are
delightful, and I've managed to make friends in the sizable
expatriate camp, mostly fellow Brits, but a few Americans as
well. The smallness of Feltre gives little divide between the
uppers and lowers, the swells and the locals. It's an agreeable

place to spend the years left to me. I read, dabble in water-colors, and keep my journal.

Each morning begins right here at the Café Ramella, one of many under the arches of the Piazza Maggiore. It's a great location for people watching, plus the family that runs the Ramella caters to the local Brits with its excellent array of teas.

It was here, on a bright, hot morning in September, that I first laid eyes on two of the most contrasting women I would ever meet. That morning, looking up from the London dailies to gaze out at the pristine Renaissance piazza, I saw them enter from the northern end, walking straight toward Café Ramella. They walked under a large, white umbrella.

Once under the arcade, the one holding the umbrella closed it, and I got my first close look at them. Penelope Lamb, who'd been holding the umbrella, was the older of the two by at least thirty years. I guessed her to be in her early seventies. She was much shorter than her friend. She was wearing a weathered pith helmet and a safari suit. Anna, her companion, was equally incongruous. She was tall, slim, raven-haired, a real stunner. She had on a haltered sundress and high-heeled sandals, her wrists covered with charm bracelets.

They took the table right next to mine, and I saw that the younger woman bore a resemblance to Ava Gardner. The older of the two looked like a classic British eccentric, a real Agatha Christie type. She was petite and fine featured, and when she sat down and removed her helmet a great lion's mane of gray hair tumbled out.

Gino, one of the owner's older sons, took their orders, making little effort to conceal his attraction for Anna. When he returned with their tea, espresso, and Continental breakfasts, he delivered a complimentary remark to Anna. She laughed and said something flirty. Penelope stared down at her lap.

When Gino went inside, the women started arguing. Anna said something in what I recognized to be Neapolitan slang.

Penelope kept her voice down, but was quite firm. After some back-and-forth, she looked to have gained the upper hand. The younger woman pouted for a while then made moves to make up. She whispered apologies and smiled sweetly. In time Penelope was patting her hand.

Peace restored, Miss Lamb, completely unperturbed, turned and introduced herself and her friend. "This is Anna. She's my assistant and my dear companion," she said. Our conversation in English excluded Anna, but she didn't seem to mind. She sipped her espresso, looked beautiful, and followed Gino's movements from table to table.

Penelope told me she and Anna lived at the Villa Adria, four miles north of Feltre. She said she was an archaeologist, retired from the field. Other than a few tidbits about her profession, she was reluctant to divulge much about herself and nothing of Anna. Most of our conversation was about Feltre, mutual expatriate friends, the weather.

When we'd been chatting for a half hour or so, Anna began to fidget with her cigarette case and purse. Penelope said they had to leave. Rather abruptly, the two stood up, walked down the steps and across the piazza beneath their big, white umbrella.

Two weeks passed before I had further contact with Miss Lamb. It came in the form of a note addressed to me at the café. It was a handwritten invitation to dinner at the villa on the forthcoming Friday—seven p.m. "promptly." I hadn't been to a dinner party in months. My own life was and is rather boring, and the idea of seeing Miss Lamb and Anna again in their home intrigued me. I sent an RSVP right away. On the appointed day, I had my hair done and put on my best dinner dress and pearls. As I didn't drive, I enlisted Gino to take me out to the villa in his old Fiat.

I'd previously glimpsed the Villa Adria on a drive with friends to Cortina. A portion of its pink roof is visible from the road, rising above the cypresses. That evening Gino turned onto the long pebbled drive that climbs up from the main road. The grounds were overgrown, and the *palazzina* itself looked like a great, pink wedding cake gone to ruin.

Expecting a bustle of cars pulling in or dropping people off, I was surprised to find the parking area empty when we reached it. I thought I must be the first to arrive. Gino offered to sit with me until other guests came, but by seven the Fiat was still the only car parked in the front oval. As the invitation made a point of underlining the word "promptly," I stepped out of the car and told Gino to come back for me at ten.

At the door, a dark-skinned man in a blue, full-length tunic greeted me. He bowed and introduced himself as Rashid, my servant for the evening. Inside everything was very English manor in decor, lots of dark wood paneling and velvet walls. We passed through a hallway to a cavernous dining room with a table capable of accommodating twenty. Penelope sat there with a setting for her and one other person.

At that point, I realized I was the only guest. Miss Lamb sensed my surprise and said she'd invited me because of my sincere and trustworthy manner. She wanted a chance to speak with me at length and share a confidence. With my curiosity piqued, I sat down and inquired as to Anna's absence. Penelope, her wild hair sticking out from under her pith helmet, wearing a wine-colored velvet evening gown, said we'd be joining Anna for dessert.

Over dinner of roast beef and Yorkshire pudding, Penelope spoke openly. I learned that the Villa Adria was a seventeenth-century *palazzina* built by Penelope's ancestors on her mother's side. She bought it from her impoverished relatives in the late '40s, after her adored mother died.

Her father had been an English lord; her mother, an Italian countess. After a brief courtship, they married and moved to England. Her parents were mismatched from the beginning, and divorced when she was old enough to be sent to boarding school. Books were her chief escape away from home. Her favorite subject was history. After reading T. E. Lawrence's *Seven Pillars of Wisdom*, she developed a passion for the Middle East. She yearned to study that vast, intriguing area in depth, so at the age of seventeen, she matriculated at Oxford. Few if any women attended university at the time, and the only reason her father agreed to finance her studies was her false promise to find a marriageable mate among the quads of ivy.

At Oxford Penelope's favorite don was an archaeologist who took her on her first field trip to Jordan. She described with great excitement her view of Petra, riding horseback through a gorge and coming out on the other side to the spectacle of rose-red buildings carved in stone. It was an epiphany.

Upon graduating, she took a post at the University of London's Department of Oriental Studies. Soon she would be working in the field, learning the "art of digging." Iraq became her base and the ancient cultures of Sumer and Babylon her focused areas of interest. Particularly fascinated by the matriarchal nature of the ancient civilizations, she became an expert on the goddess Inanna, the earliest incarnation of Isis, Aphrodite, and Venus. Inanna was worshipped in the Tigris–Euphrates valley as the creator and source of universal order, presiding over a world where women bought and sold property and inheritance was passed from mother to daughter.

Away from work, Penelope avoided Europeans and penetrated the indigenous culture. It was a dangerous undertaking for a woman. She had to dress like a native, her face and body concealed in a black burnoose with a small slit to peer through. But she was successful. She gained confidence and trust in the closed society of Iraqi women. Sitting with them in their harems made her feel transported to ancient times. The sensation was especially strong when she was in the company of the degraded women of Baghdad's streets. She befriended them, took them into her house, fed and clothed them, and made certain they were clean and healthy. To Penelope they were descendants of the courtesans who once reigned over the very temples she was digging.

In time, Penelope was recognized for her expertise and knowledge. She wrote a book, *Inanna: Queen of Heaven*, still considered the ultimate source on the matriarchal dawn of the Middle East.

It was at that point, her reputation and eminence secured, that Miss Lamb uncovered her most important cache. She was digging in a temple in Uruk, digging deeper and deeper, back into time, deeper than anyone had dug before, when she came upon a completely intact statue of Inanna, the first ever excavated.

The custom for archaeologists then, as now, was to excavate and document their findings, then turn them over to the national museum of the host country—in Miss Lamb's case, the Republic of Iraq. Once that procedure was completed, institutions and archeologists could bid on their findings. Knowing that the museum in Iraq would never give up the statue of Inanna, Penelope decided to break the law. Risking career, reputation, and criminal prosecution, she smuggled the statue out of the country.

When dinner was consumed, Penelope rose and said it was time to join Anna. She led me through a door off the dining room, down a stairwell to her personal museum. "Everything you see here, with one exception, was legally obtained," she said, "bought at great cost and well documented." The room was crammed with cases of artifacts, like the old rooms at the British Museum I'd visited as a child. Everything was of Sumerian origin. The bounty must have been worth millions.

"Let me show you my secret treasure," she said. The statue of Inanna stood under a soft cone of light in a recess. It was alabaster, pure white, less than a foot high, without a single crack. Its voluptuous figure was evident beneath a carved, pleated dress. Both hands held a gold cup. Its most striking feature was its disproportionately large eyes. They were other-worldly, gazing with fixed awe on a point in the night sky, replicated on the ceiling.

Penelope said that for many years she worshipped the silent, immovable stone. It was the embodiment of the world she wished she had been born into. Then something marvelous happened. Stone turned to flesh.

"Let me show you," she said.

We entered a deeper chamber. It had a low table surrounded by pillows on an Oriental carpet. The table was spread with dishes of savories. There was a pool with a fountain and petals floating on the surface. On the far side of the pool, seated on a regal chair, was Anna.

I almost gasped! She was dressed exactly like the statue of Inanna. With both hands she held a gold cup, and her kohl-lined eyes looked upward with a fixed stare at the ceiling. Once we were seated on the pillows, Penelope raised her own gold cup, filled with an unidentifiable liquid, and offered praise to Anna/Inanna. "Queen of Heaven, Divine Inanna, Courtesan of the Gods of Fire, Water, Storm, and Wind." Composed and unspeaking, Anna remained seated on her throne. I thought she must be drugged or hypnotized. Half of me wanted to flee and half of me was enthralled. I felt queasy, as though I was observing something forbidden. I glanced at my watch. Thankfully, the hour was approaching ten. With disbelief, I asked Penelope where she met Anna.

I was told that they found each other in Naples. It was just after Penelope returned from her first visit to Pompeii. The day was brutally hot, and Penelope sat down at an open-air café to have a cool drink. Anna was walking back and forth in front of the café. She was a scruffy street girl in a tight dress and heels so high she could hardly walk. Penelope said she reminded her of the women of the street in Bagdad, the reincarnations of the temple courtesans. She reached out and grabbed Anna's hand. Anna cursed and pulled away. Penelope gave her lire and told her there would be more if she sat with her. Anna had been on the streets since she was twelve and she'd experienced just about everything—everything but an eccentric old woman in a pith helmet. Hesitantly, she came in off the street and sat down.

After a good meal, wine, and more lire, Anna began to relax. When they finished eating, they went back to Penelope's hotel. Anna had her first bath in weeks and fell asleep on the biggest, softest bed she'd ever slept in. Over the next few days they shopped, went to movies and restaurants. For Anna, it was a holiday. On her last night in Naples, Penelope asked Anna if she would come back with her to the Villa Adria. She said she'd take care of her and make sure she wanted for nothing. Anna had grown used to luxury and Penelope's generosity by then, so she agreed.

ANNA HADN'T MOVED SINCE WE SAT down. It was five to ten. I'd heard and seen as much as I could absorb in one night. I said I had to leave. Penelope escorted me to the front door, all the while thanking me for allowing her to share her secret. She said she trusted me and asked that I not betray her confidence.

When we opened the front door, I was never happier to see Gino. Penelope, however, was shocked by his presence. "What's he doing here?" she asked. I told her I didn't drive, didn't own a car, couldn't afford a chauffeur, and if it weren't for Gino, I wouldn't have accepted her invitation.

I WOULDN'T SEE PENELOPE AND ANNA again until Gordon French's Thanksgiving party. Gordon is the American architect who's built a sprawling "California modern" ranch in the hills not far from Villa Adria. That year Gordon hosted a huge gathering of expatriates and locals. Gino and I drove up together. Gordon is known for never sparing an expense, so there was no end of food and drink. Holiday lights lit up the house, indoors and out, and guests wandered the grounds.

As the afternoon drifted into evening, I saw Penelope walking by in a frantic state. She'd gotten separated from Anna. Someone told her Anna was in the carport with Gino. Penelope caught up with them and a big row ensued. Gino tried to settle things but threw up his arms and walked away. Penelope sat down on the concrete, reduced to sobbing. Anna wouldn't calm down. When Penelope said it was time to leave, Anna refused to go. Penelope sulked off to her Bentley with Rashid at the wheel. Anna stayed on, leaving with Gino and me when it was time to go. They dropped me off at my apartment before continuing on together.

After the party, the weather turned cold and I stayed in for a few weeks. When I returned to Café Ramella, Gino wasn't there. His father said he'd gone off with the signorina from Villa Adria. There were more members of the Ramella family in Venice, and that's where they hoped to settle and start a family.

I saw Penelope once at the café before I left for my annual stay in Venice. She was sitting alone, disorganized and distracted. She was wearing her pith helmet and safari suit, both soiled and unkempt, her hair wilder than ever and unwashed. I asked if I could join her. I think she would have said yes to anyone. She had a pot of tea in front of her and kept opening and closing her satchel, removing maps and keys then putting them back. She also was chain-smoking cigarettes, something that I'd never seen her do.

There was a stack of guidebooks in front of her: *Baedeker's Egypt*, as well as his guides to Morocco, Turkey, Spain, and India. She'd open one, leaf through it, then put it down and pick up another. I asked if she was planning a trip. She said as soon as she closed the villa for the winter she'd be taking an extended vacation. She said she hadn't been sleeping or eating, and no one would tell her where to find Gino and Anna. In a fit of anger, she'd thrown out all of Anna's things, including her Inanna dress and jewelry. Then she started to cry and asked if I thought that wasn't a mistake. Maybe Anna would come back. What could I say? Before I left, I told her I'd be staying in Venice through the spring. I gave her my Venetian and Feltre addresses and told her to write me.

One night shortly after arriving, I ran into Gino and Anna while sharing a water taxi. They were happy and seemed very much in love. Gino was thrilled to see me. Anna, I think, was a bit embarrassed. Gino told me he was working in the family's Venetian restaurant. I was invited to come at any time, "no expense." He said he and Anna had an apartment and planned to marry. The water taxi dropped me off before their stop. As I waved goodbye, I noticed a little bump under Anna's dress, indicating that she was in 'a family way.'

During my stay in Venice, I received countless postcards from a drifting Penelope, always with a poste restante address for her next destination. There were cards from the Alhambra, Marrakesh, Cairo, Luxor. Her handwriting was almost illegible, a scrawl of crazy impressions. Her mind seemed to be wandering just like she was. With each card, however, disjointed her descriptions and reflections, she always managed to inquire about Anna. Had I seen her? Did I know where she was? Naturally, I was mum, being as respectful of Gino and Anna's confidence as I was of Penelope's.

Once back in Feltre, I continued to receive postcards, but now Penelope's handwriting was a bit clearer, as were her thoughts. The cards were coming from Turkey, a country she'd fallen in love with. She said she found it so festive and colorful. She was travelling all over the country. I received cards from Cappadocia, Izmit, Troy, and Smyrna, all of them applauding the food, the people, the architecture, and the mix of religions.

Back in Istanbul her wanderings finally came to a halt. She loved the seat of the Ottoman Empire on the Bosphoros. I received cards from the Blue Mosque, Hagia Sophia, and Topkapi Palace. Rather than take a hotel room, she'd rented an apartment. The postcards finally ceased, as did her inquiries about Anna. Instead, I began to receive letters on a weekly basis.

She was becoming immersed in a study of the city's history. She was ministering to the young street girls, bringing them into her home to make sure they were fed, clean, and healthy. When she'd been in Istanbul for several months, I received a letter saying she was returning to Feltre.

I was here at the Café Ramella, on a bright, hot morning in September, looking up from the London dailies to gaze out at the pristine Piazza Maggiore, when I saw Penelope, in her pith helmet and safari suit, enter the piazza from the northern end with a much younger woman. They were walking straight toward me, under a large, white umbrella.

Once under the arches Penelope unfurled her umbrella. She was much changed from the woman I'd last seen at the café. She was calm and composed with a healthy glow on her face and a twinkle in her bright blue eyes. "I'd like you to meet Fatima," she said. "She's from Istanbul. She's come to live with me at the villa and be my companion."

# The Serenity of the Scholar

AMONG THE PERSONAL PAPERS OTTO RITSCHL brought with him from Germany to the Institute for Advanced Studies in 1933 was a letter from his former mentor, Franz Neurohr. Written during a lucid interlude several years after his admittance to Brinswagner Asylum, the letter was an attempt by the famous classicist to recall the events preceding the apoplectic fit that initiated his breakdown.

The following portion of the letter appeared shortly after Ritschl's death in J. M. Montfort's *Freiburg to Brinswagner: A Critical Life of Franz Neurohr* (Princeton University Press,1951).

AT DAWN ON MY FORTY-FOURTH BIRTHDAY, I left my rooms in the vicinity of the Piazza Carlo Alberto and headed for the Ponte Vittorio Emanuele. The chill autumn wind off the Po was so biting that I shivered as I walked, pulling my coat tightly around me. Since arriving in Turin the previous August, I had taken to having a constitutional each morning, and in the fortnight prior to my birthday, the walks commenced at the earliest possible hour. A terrible dream was waking me in the middle of the night, its contents of such a disturbing nature that I could not regain sleep once wakened. Starved of rest, at sunrise I was eager to quit my rooms to find fresh air and open spaces.

As I crossed the bridge to the right bank of the Po, the snowy peaks of the Alps came into view, ringing the city in a blinding white crescent. A muddy track ran along the riverbank. On this path I waked north, with the headache and nausea that followed my nightmare still persisting. Sharp pains drummed in my brow whenever I looked up in the direction of the mountains, and in an effort to relieve my discomfort, I removed my glasses and massaged my eyes. In so doing, the rays of sunshine passing through my eyelids became the blood of the murdered horse of my dream—the old sad workhorse, pursued by a mob through the shadowy streets of an unfamiliar town, pursued until it was trapped in a square and stoned.

Each time the dream recurred I saw myself within it, standing naked, bending over the dying animal. In my extended hand I offered a tuft of dry grass. Past caring for food, the horse sighed deeply, not accepting my offering. A man brandishing a kitchen knife then stepped forth from the crowd. Slowly and deliberately, he knelt down beside the horse, and with one swift stroke, he slashed its throat. After the butchery, blood flowed over the stones in the square and the man turned to the spectators, signaling them to draw near so they might drink of the warm liquid. Always, at that moment, night after night, I bolted from my sleep, gasping for air, feeling as though a succubus was crushing my chest.

A few hours of waking beside the Po led me far from town and into the Piedmont. The alpine air and mountain peaks towering over clusters of oak and beech had a beneficent effect. A kindly farmer in his field offered me a cup of fiery grappa, and with its ingestion, my pains and nausea subsided. By midday, compelled by ravenous hunger, I hastened back to the city.

Beneath the arcade facing the Piazza Carlo Alberto, I sat at a window table in the little trattoria at which I was accustomed to eating. The light of the early afternoon lengthened the shadow cast by the piazza's statue and deepened the yellow and reddish brown of the encircling buildings' facades. I ordered soup, trout, and a bottle of Barolo. As I waited for the meal to be brought to the table, a feeling of warmth and well-being coursed through my body. It was a sensation I attributed to the favorableness of Turin. The city's elegant architecture, the bracing mountain climate, the hearty cuisine, and the generous spirit of the people served as a restorative to normal vigor after the tumultuous years at Freiburg, years beginning at the age of twenty-five, when I first assumed the responsibilities of the chair of Classical Philology. The endless lectures, obligatory publications, and arguments with colleagues over the future of art and serious thinking made Freiburg a cauldron, not a sanctuary for scholarly endeavor. After two decades of demanding work and intense cerebration I was rewarded not with praise and recognition but with chronically poor health, failing vision, and a state of near-total exhaustion.

Sitting in the trattoria, I was grateful for my forced retirement. The move to Turin made me free at last of the burdens of the academy, finally free to be the unyoked poet and philosopher I yearned to be. As I was about to commit these thoughts to a pocket notebook, I was distracted by the sound of a commotion in the center of the square. Looking out the window, I saw a cab driver stopping to give his balking horse a vicious beating. Overwhelmed with pity, I raced to the tortured animal. I threw my arms around its neck and collapsed.

# *Espresso Cinecittá*

"Silence on the set!" Giordano Giorgi barked into his megaphone. In Cinecittà's Theatre 14 he was ready to roll the cameras on the brothel scene in his new film.

"*Silenzio!*"

The din and frenzy of the movie set diminished to a hush. The crew froze in position with their eyes on the great director.

On the set, a nymph in a ruffled nightgown sat on a swing in the brothel's sitting room. A fat, bearded madam stood behind a bar with a flashing neon heart pinned to her breast. A rouged and powdered female midget reclined amid soapsuds in a marble tub.

From his swivel seat, high on a platform over the set, Giorgi shouted to his assistants milling below. "Guido! Where are the rest of the whores?! Two dozen whores are scripted for this scene! And the arc lights, Angelo! They're angled all wrong!"

Guido and Angelo were set in feverish motion.

Giorgi bellowed at the art director. "*Dio bastardo*, Ettore! Why aren't the fans blowing on the paper flames? They're hanging there like limp tulips!"

Ettore ran to the electric fans.

Giorgi swiveled on the platform and pointed his megaphone toward a slim, elegant young woman standing away from the bustle of activity. "Claudia!" he shouted to his publicist niece. "Where's Vincenzo? Why is that bastard not on the set?"

Unlike his other frantic and terrorized aides, Claudia was all poise and quiet cool. Her raven hair was pixie cut and she wore a lime-green Milano ensemble. She smiled up at her raging uncle with youthful self-confidence. "Ah, *mio zio*, there's a little problem."

"A little problem, Claudia? There are no little problems in a big movie with a monster budget and the most expensive leading man in Europe! Where *is* that son of a bitch?"

"Uncle Giordano, Vincenzo's under the weather. It's taking him a little extra time to look presentable for the take."

"You mean he's hungover?!" roared Giorgi. "Was the bastard out all night again with the American *puttana*?!"

Claudia feigned disapproval. "If you're referring to Mona Carlson, Uncle, she's a rising star in Hollywood. She's making a big splash in Rome."

"*Si*, like the splash she made the other night jumping into Ettore's pool in her underwear. That stunt made all the tabloids. Did you ever see one of her films? *Cigarette Girls*? *Valley of Vixens*? Jesus! I thought she was supposed to be in Spain, playing a shepherdess in Nick Ray's Bible epic."

"They're having problems, *zio*. All the tech people are on strike. Filming has come to a halt. Mona's taking advantage of the break to be seen on the Via Veneto. And why not? The eyes of the world are on the Italian film industry."

"*Porco Dio!* Stop with the PR clichés! She's running Vincenzo ragged. He thinks he's a teenager, but the wrinkles in his face say otherwise."

"But think of the attention, *zio*! The paparazzi are going crazy over Vincenzo and Mona in the cafés and clubs at night.

Their pictures are in all the papers and magazines. And not just the Italian press. It's big news all over Europe and the States. Wonderful publicity for your film!"

Giorgi groaned. "Dearest Claudia, only child of my crazy sister, I'm shooting my personal version of the *Inferno*, what you've rightly dubbed 'my most ambitious project to date'; and to my eternal suffering, my very own Dante, the star of the film, picks for his real-life love interest a dizzy tart with a brain as tiny as a peach pit! She has him on a steady diet of champagne and dancing till dawn. They say he won a twist contest last night! I'll twist his goddamned neck when I see him. He's losing his mind!"

Claudia laughed. "So you read my description of the *Inferno*. That was in my last press release. It will be your masterpiece, *zio*. You'll make them forget about Godard and Bergman!"

"I'm not so sure. Godard's hell has to be talked about and talked about. The French! So cerebral. And Bergman has his cold, dark shadows, his brooding Nordic hell of interior landscapes. He's my polar opposite. I'll create a hell with beautiful souls on fire, the rival of anything either has done!"

While her uncle mused on the poignancy of his cinematic insights, Claudia saw Vincenzo Valentini stumble from his dressing room into the melee of Theatre 14 dressed in a schoolboy's outfit of short pants, kneesocks, a starched white shirt, and a striped necktie reaching halfway to his waistline. The makeup artist had not quite obscured the dark rings under his eyes or altered his drawn expression. At forty-three, Vincenzo was a sad-eyed, handsome man.

When Claudia was a schoolgirl and Vincenzo a rising star, she'd had an enormous crush on him, but that was over now. In the years since, she'd grown up and had her own real love affairs. She'd been to university and come to work for her famous uncle. She'd also gotten to see the real Valentini. Without stardust in her eyes, she'd taken his measure and found him lacking. Still, he was so beautiful. Sad, too. That was all part of his charm.

Claudia caught Vincenzo's eye and quickly walked over to him while her uncle fretted with the lighting man. "Uncle Giordano is furious!" She spoke in an undertone so that no one would hear her. "Your morning-after problems are holding up production."

Bloodshot and sleepy, Vincenzo flashed his reflexive rake's grin. "Ah, Claudia, if only I had a woman with steel in her spine like you to take care of me, I wouldn't have to stray."

"Oh please, Vincenzo. You're supposed to be Dante, not Don Giovanni."

"There you are, you bastard!" screamed Giorgi. "You look like hell."

"Hell's what this movie's about. You don't want me to look like a rosy-cheeked grocer's son."

"You look like Dracula's grandfather, *bastardo*. Are you prepared for the brothel scene?"

"Of course, *mio Maestro*." Vincenzo removed his schoolboy cap and bowed.

"Then step on the set and let's get on with it!"

Slowly, the leading actor of Italian cinema moved to his marks while the required actresses swarmed to their places before the bearded madam and the midget in the tub. Blondes and redheads took their positions, brunettes and black-haired vamps, women in various states of dress and undress. A nun stood next to a dominatrix. A belly dancer undulated past a librarian. A goggled aviatrix and a squaw in buckskin danced in a circle with an African woman wearing little more than an orange turban. A buttoned and corseted Victorian bumped up against a maid in black net stockings. Nudes walked in and out of the action with nonchalance.

In the center of the scene stood the absurdly dressed Vincenzo, his attention focused on the film's Beatrice, the nightgowned girl in the swing, Dante's image of love and innocent desire.

The set lights glowed, the cameras rolled, and Vincenzo moved in and spoke his lines, atrociously.

"*Cut!*" howled Giorgi. "You'll have to do better, Vincenzo."

Technicians, actors, and assorted assistants set up again. The clap sticks snapped. The girl swung languorously. And Vincenzo messed up again.

"*Cut!* There's no magic, no magic. It's dead!" shouted Giordano.

Repeatedly, the action stopped and started again. They made twenty-eight attempts to film the scene with nothing to show for it but two dozen women sweating profusely, their makeup running under the lights. Grim-faced assistants toiled under Giorgi's glare and Vincenzo Valentini grew ever more fatigued. The man who'd twice won the Actor's Prize at Cannes missed his marks repeatedly and flubbed his lines like an amateur. Trying to gaze soulfully at the girl in the swing, he broke up laughing more than once.

As the possibility for a successful scene crumbled before his eyes, Giordano Giorgi grew more and more discouraged, his energy deflated. After saying "*Cut*" on the thirty-first take, the director ordered everyone to close up shop for the day.

Beatrice wept softly in her swing. Giorgi let out a long, slow sigh. Vincenzo volunteered to try again but Giordano waved him away. "*Basta!* Enough. You haven't got it today. I'm tired. I need food, wine and an evening away from Cinecittà. Tomorrow we'll make movies the right way. Today's *finito*."

As production broke up and equipment was packed and rolled away, Claudia sat in the shadows, deep in thought. She was ambitious and determined to succeed in the male-dominated world of Italian cinema. She burned to produce and direct and power-play on the Via Veneto, just like her uncle, but it would be a long, hard climb for Giordano Giorgi's pretty little niece. Being Cinecittà's best publicist—and she knew she was, regardless of her youth—wasn't enough. She had to find other ways to prove herself. She had to find a way to assist her uncle in an area where he most needed assistance. Her drive was making her clock tick faster and faster.

She sat in her canvas chair with her legs crossed and smiled. There was a way. There was a way. *Casting!* God knows her uncle needed help in that department, and she knew most of the young actors and actresses in Rome. She'd become a star-maker; she'd pick and choose from the local talent to meet the growing demand for Italians on the screen at home and abroad. That would impress her uncle and move her up the Cinecittà ladder.

She went over to where her uncle stood alone, drinking San Pellegrino in glum meditation. "Cheer up, *zio*. One fucked-up day can't kill a movie like Giorgi's *Inferno!*"

Her uncle shook his finger. "Watch your mouth. You sound like a gangster moll."

Claudia laughed. "You mean I sound like you! Listen, Uncle, I think I have an answer to your problems."

Giordano gave her a heavy-lidded look. "You're a smart girl, Claudia, but you'd have to be Einstein or Eisenstein to fix this pain in my balls."

She took his hand and whispered. "It's Vincenzo, *zio*. He's not right for Dante. He's too old. Don't look at me like that! You know it's true, better than I do! Listen, he'll be around making movies when he's sixty! He's like James Stewart and Cary Grant in that way. But he's not Italy's great heartthrob anymore. He's let his lust for booze and skirts pull him down." Her lips moved close to her uncle's ear. "He's not right for this film! He's making a mockery of your vision! The critics will pan him, unmercifully, and the public will stay away from the box office when they see how he's slipped."

"*Porco Madonna!* What do I do with an *Inferno* without Dante? Vincenzo's my star. He's been with me from the beginning. I know he's a lush and can't keep his pants on, but I can't kick him out the door and pull in someone new off the street."

Claudia squeezed both his hands tightly. "Not off the street, *zio*. I have just the actor in mind. He's a waiter at one of your favorite haunts, Café Limbo!"

Giorgi rolled his eyes. "Mother of Christ! Just like that you've discovered a younger version of Vincenzo at the Limbo? No bum of a waiter is going to step in and play Dante!"

"This waiter will! Tonight I'll introduce you. His name is Sandro Donati. He's a brilliant young actor in a little avant garde theater group. Don't laugh. He's wonderful and almost as good-looking as Vincenzo when *he* started out! Ahhh, now you look interested! You'll see. You'll see, *zio*. Tonight at Café Limbo."

"Okay, okay. I'll meet your heartthrob of a waiter. If he brings me good food and doesn't behave like a *gavone*, I'll leave him a big tip."

Claudia clapped her hands and gave a little leap in her white Courrèges boots. It's little me that's giving *you* the big tip, she thought.

LATER THAT EVENING CLAUDIA PARKED HER Alfa Romeo and joined Giorgi with his entourage as they walked the Via Veneto. Giordano sported a black fedora and a too-tight suit stretched against his large frame. Claudia wore a coral-pink outfit to fit her exuberant mood—a mini-dress and heels, with matching accessories. Her dangling earrings reflected the headlights and streetlamps around her. As they approached Café Limbo, a pack of paparazzi descended on Giorgi and bombarded him with questions.

"*Maestro! Maestro!* Why all the delays with the *Inferno*?"

"Are you losing control of production, *Maestro*?"

Claudia jumped in front of her uncle and assumed her role as his primary link to the press. Responding to their insistent questions and wisecracks was something she did with relish.

"Hey, Claudia! What's the scoop on Vincenzo and Mona Carlson? Will they be here tonight?"

"Check out her pink mini! Why don't you step out from behind the cameras and become an actress, Claudia?"

"Nah! She's too flat chested!"

Claudia kicked the joker with a sharp-tipped shoe and laughed. "Don't worry about Giorgi's *Inferno*. One hundred years from now they'll be talking about this film. It will be the crown jewel of Italian cinema!" They jotted down her words as she walked and talked. "As for me, I have no pretensions about acting. I do my best work behind the scenes."

Giorgi's group walked in through the Limbo's leather doors in a hail of flashes. The maître d' made a little bow to the great director and guided the group swiftly to their usual table. It was tucked in a semi private dining space, separated from the dance floor by a row of fake palms and a trellis of silk ivy.

The Limbo was vibrant with café society. Hooligans mingled with the bohemian chic in a pleasure seeker's democracy. Monte Carlo moguls dined with street hustlers. A welterweight contender danced with an heiress. The *Inferno* party settled into their seats to see and be seen.

A short, bald waiter took orders all around as Claudia's eyes searched the nightclub for a sign of Sandro. She ordered an Americano while Giorgi talked shop with his art director.

"Don't tell the producers, Ettore." He winked. "But in a way I'm glad the whorehouse shoot went down the toilet today. I misconceived the scene. Valentini did me a favor by showing up half in the bag."

"You're thinking of scrapping the bordello scene?!" Ettore asked incredulously.

"Not scrapping it. It's the piéce de résistance of the film. Let's put it on the shelf and let it marinate. We're adding a brand-new scene. It's not in the screenplay. It was born in a dream I had last night. . ."

As her uncle recounted his dream, Claudia tapped her foot, looking about, anxiously. Where was Sandro? Other waiters brought stuffed artichokes and batter-fried strips of salt cod, but not Sandro. The table talk buzzed as she kept scanning the club.

"In the new scene, Virgil will lead Dante through a desolate landscape to a castle on a hill—something out of Frankenstein or Kane's Xanadu . . ."

Baby lamb chops came to the table with saltimbocca, red and white wine, and *crostini alla provatura*. Claudia asked a waiter softly where Sandro might be.

"In the dream I had a perfect vision of hell's seventh circle—the corruption of art. The castle's the home of a famous painter. He's lost his soul. He's old, fat, ugly, and dwells in a tower in his studio tomb. The room is cluttered with cobwebbed canvases and paint pots. Dozens of unfinished oils stand against the walls. The artist is surrounded by sycophants, parasites who kiss his ass and live off his wealth like vampires."

"*Scusi*, zio." Claudia got up from the table and walked into the café's busy kitchen. There by the staff lockers sat her boyfriend of three weeks, Sandro Donati. He was reading the latest issue of *Cahiers du Cinema* with avid concentration.

"*Dio mio!* Are you out of your mind, Sandro? Uncle Giordano's out in the dining room and you sit here reading a magazine!"

Sandro looked up dreamily at his exasperated girlfriend. He had a face like Belmondo's, only with smaller features and black-framed glasses. "In this issue there's a review of Godard's *Les Caribiniers*, Buster Keaton's *The General*, and a great piece on Nicholas Ray. Did you know he's shooting in Spain?"

"Jesus! My uncle's here and I'm about to make you a star! Why aren't you in your waiter's outfit?"

"Pietro. He just fired me for being late again. I'm through with waiting anyway. I never liked this shit hole.

Getting ordered about by a bunch of assholes! I'm an artist, not a servant."

Claudia glared. "Yes, you're an artist! That's why I want you to meet my uncle, so you'll be recognized. Don't you want to meet Giordano Giorgi and get the big break you've wanted?!"

"Of course, *bambina*. But if I step out on the floor, Pietro will throw me out. He thinks I left hours ago. I've been hiding back here hoping you'd find me."

Claudia threw up her hands. "What a screwup! Uncle's holding court, and we'll spoil his evening if you get in a row with the owner." She clenched her teeth and banged her fist on Sandro's knees. "Look. I'll give you a pass to Theatre 14 for tomorrow. Wear a clean shirt and a sports jacket. And please wear your contact lenses. These glasses make you look like a math teacher!"

Sandro shrugged. "I lost the lenses, *bambina*."

"Shit! Just show up at Theatre 14 first thing in the morning. See that that broken down Fiat of yours gets you to the lot."

"Can't you pick me up?"

Claudia balanced Sandro's glasses on the bridge of his nose and gave him a quick kiss. "I have other things to do. Important things. It's all part of my plan."

"*Sì*, your plan, your mysterious master plan. You're always plotting something."

She kissed him again. "Just be at Theatre 14 tomorrow. It'll all work out."

Sandro left by the back door and Claudia rejoined the party. Espresso was being served and Signor Giorgi looked contented and well fed. He was telling tales expansively when Vincenzo and Mona Carlson swept into the club.

Mona was a voluptuous lavender illusion with coiffed bouffant blondness. She floated to the table in chiffon, aware of the eyes following her progress.

Vincenzo made introductions as the house band struck up "Patricia." "Giordano, it's my pleasure to introduce you to Miss Mona Carlson. She's America's answer to Anita Ekberg!"

Giorgi eyed Valentini balefully then stood up and kissed Mona's outstretched hand. "And a lovely answer she is."

Mona giggled. Her voice was one part Marilyn and one part ineradicable Bronx. "It's a pleasure to make your acquaintance, Mr. Giorgi. From what everyone tells me, you're a real artist."

"Alas, I can't claim such stature, Signorina," Giorgi said with a large dollop of false modesty. "Ingmar Bergman is a real artist. Are you familiar with his films?"

Mona was puzzled but determined to impress the famous director. "Of course," she lied. "I've seen all of them, Mr. Giorgi, but they can't compare to yours."

Giorgi smiled at Mona's attempt at sincerity and invited her and Vincenzo to join the table. Mona took a seat next to Claudia.

"This is Claudia Giorgi," Vincenzo said, "the Maestro's niece and a little sister to me. She's also one hell of a PR girl, so watch what you say to her. Hey, Giancarlo!" Vincenzo caught sight of an old buddy at another table and ran over to say hello.

"Mona, I'm so excited to meet you! You're the hottest thing in Hollywood!"

"I guess you'd know," said Mona. "Vincenzo says you're hip to all the inside goings-on in the business."

"I try to keep up," chimed Claudia. "You were a knockout in *Cigarette Girls*. That strip scene really put you on the map!"

"Yeah, I guess everyone liked what they saw," said Mona sarcastically.

"It must be great shooting in Spain with Nick Ray."

"Are you kidding?" Mona gagged. "It's too hot, the hotel's a dump, and the food is lousy. To top it off, nobody speaks English. Not that I got anything against Spaniards." Mona moved closer and spoke as one woman of the world to another. "I did meet a bullfighter. He wasn't disappointing."

The two put their heads together and laughed. "Seriously," Claudia said unseriously, "you're doing the right thing by making this Bible film with Nick Ray. You don't want to get typecast like Mansfield."

Mona nodded eagerly. "That's exactly what I told my agent! Show the world I'm a serious actress."

The house band was cooking, playing "The Twist," as they lead up to their signature limbo rituals.

Before Vincenzo swept Mona away, Claudia set up phase two of her plan. "Mona, I know you're on your way to achieving the serious acclaim you deserve, and I have some further suggestions that I think you'll be very interested in. But I can't discuss them here. There's too much distraction." She leaned over and squeezed Mona's hand. "How would you like it if I picked you up at the Grand Hotel tomorrow morning for a special tour of Cinecittà? You can watch Uncle shoot the *Inferno*. On the drive out, I'll tell you about my ideas."

Mona responded with a conspiratorial smile, amid cigarette smoke, party noise, and rock 'n' roll. "I like you, Claudia. You're the type who's always thinking. I'd like to know what you've got up your sleeve."

Claudia smiled winningly at her new friend and confidant. "I'll pick you up at ten sharp. Don't stay out too late with Valentini!"

Mona glanced at Giorgi's Dante returning to the table. "It's a deal, Claudia. Vincenzo's ready to collapse anyway. See you at ten." The two women shook hands and said good night before Vincenzo grabbed Mona and pulled her out to the dance floor.

Giorgi puffed blue cigar plumes and pushed away his dessert plate. "What happened to your heartthrob waiter, Claudia? The guys serving this table look like Akim Tamiroff and Peter Lorre."

Claudia picked at her long-cold saltimbocca. "Wouldn't you know it! His Fiat broke down! He never made it to work, but I assure you he'll be at Cinecittà tomorrow. Better anyway! Better to see him away from this commotion."

Caribbean strains sounded from the dance floor.

Giordano patted his stomach. "*Porco bastardo!* Do you actually think my film's success could be salvaged by a waiter with a rundown Fiat? With all due respect, you're crazier than your mother!"

Claudia stuck her tongue out at her uncle and pointed to the dance area. "Look, *zio*! Vincenzo's doing the limbo."

With his back arched and knees bent, Valentini was trying to maneuver under a horizontal bamboo pole held three feet above the floor. His face was flushed and sweaty as he moved to calypso rhythms. A crowd circled around him, laughing and cheering. "Lower!" they shouted. "Lower! Lower!"

Giordano Giorgi shook his head and muttered under his breath. Mona was clapping her hands, cheering Vincenzo on. Claudia took everything in with a determined smile on her face.

"Lower!" the crowd chanted. "Lower! Lower! Lower!"

THE FOLLOWING MORNING, CLAUDIA ENTERED THE Grand Hotel as scheduled. She was as stylish as ever, wearing pencil-thin black capris and a black and white polka dot blouse. Tipped off by Claudia, journalists were already waiting in the lobby. They sprang into action when Mona Carlson stepped out of the elevator in a light blue sundress, showing lots of leg and cleavage. She greeted Claudia with an air kiss and feigned indifference to the news hounds.

"Mona! Are you and Valentini engaged?"

"Are you making a deal to star in a Giordano Giorgi film?"

The newsmen kept up their barrage as the two women walked out of the lobby.

"Do you sleep in the nude, Mona?"

"How do Italian men stack up as lovers?"

"Tell us about your role as a shepherdess in Nick Ray's new movie!"

Mona stopped before the large wrought-iron doors, turned, and faced the pack. "Listen! Here's the scoop of the century! Mona Carlson confesses she takes showers in the nude! Totally nude! Totally, totally, totally nude!" With that she spun around on her heels, grabbed Claudia by the elbow, and walked outside.

The pair hurried to Claudia's Alfa convertible. In the clear morning air, with both driver and passenger wearing head-scarves and sunglasses, the car pulled out into traffic.

"So what do you think of Rome, Mona? Exciting enough for you?"

"It beats Spain, honey. The paparazzi are really wild! I have a tan from the flashbulbs." Mona smiled over her shoulder at the press car following in close pursuit.

"Cinecittà's where it's all happening. There's nothing else like it in Europe. Only Hollywood can compare in importance."

"L.A.'s dull next to Rome. After slaving all day at the studios there's nothing to do at night. No club life. Nothing like Café Limbo. Everyone goes to bed early so they can wake up ready to start making more money."

"*Si*, but what about all the young, sexy actors? They must keep you busy!"

Mona munched on her gum. "I've had some fun. But you'd be surprised at how many of the big box-office guys are total bores, especially in bed."

"Nothing surprises me, *amica*. How do you like Vincenzo?"

"He's a doll, but he drinks too much. When it's time for bed, he passes out."

Claudia laughed. "It's all the pressure he's under making my uncle's film. At his age, it's not the right part for him. He'd be great in light, romantic stuff. But Dante's *Inferno*? Forget it! Confidentially, I suspect he knows he's in over his head, and I suspect my uncle would like to see someone else in the role. Uncle just doesn't have the heart to can Vincenzo."

"Really?" Mona sounded genuinely surprised.

"It's true," said Claudia, weaving in and out of lanes as she sped toward the eastern outskirts of the city. "Vincenzo's still the biggest male lead in Europe. But Uncle's movie is going to make him look bad, and that will make Uncle look bad. That's what I really wanted to talk to you about."

"Me? What can I do?"

Behind her shades Claudia flashed a dark-eyed glance at Mona. "You do realize that you and Vincenzo are the hottest pair in all the tabloids and fanzines. Since you two hit it off, the press can't get enough!"

"Vincenzo and I aren't serious. It's a fling, something to keep me busy while I'm waiting for things to pick up in Spain."

"I understand, but the world doesn't see it that way. Everybody thinks this is Taylor and Burton all over again!"

"You're putting me on."

"Let me put it this way, you two together are bigger than the sum of your parts." Claudia breezed on. "This is Hollywood marries Cinecittà! What a combination! You two eloping will make the story of the year!"

Mona almost swallowed her Chiclets. "Eloping! Claudia, honey, you're out of your mind! I'm not gonna elope with Vincenzo. He can't get it up half the time!"

"Easy, easy, *amica*. Sex has nothing to do with it. This is about careers. Without Vincenzo you've got third billing in a low-budget Bible flick. After a headline elopement, you'll be box-office dynamite!"

Mona listened carefully as Claudia spelled out her stratagem. "In a couple of days, you and Vincenzo disappear. I start feeding rumors to the news. The suspense builds and production stops on the *Inferno*. Stories start swirling about a double-star kidnapping. . ."

They passed the cinder-block apartment buildings off the Appia Nuova and approached the Cinecittà studios, still trailed by a carful of paparazzi.

"Then we shoot the scoop all over the world! You two turn up somewhere on the Amalfi coast on your honeymoon. It turns out you were married in a little church with no one in attendance but the priest and his sainted mother!"

"And what happens to your uncle's film?"

"To begin with, Uncle fires Valentini for breach of contract. Vincenzo resigns in the name of love. You finish up a quickie honeymoon, with the world press peeping in your bedroom window. You return to Spain with your big catch. The producers decide your film is top budget. After all, you're married to Europe's leading actor. You move from third to first billing!"

"Over Stephen Boyd!"

"Over Stephen Boyd. Movie fans can't wait for the Bible epic's release!"

"Yeah, but without Vincenzo does the *Inferno* go down the drain?"

"No, no! Uncle is privately delighted. He's got Vincenzo out of his hair. Now he can make a true director's film. No more star system. All unknowns in the cast!"

"Whew!" Mona digested the plan and grinned broadly, showing a full set of porcelain crowns. "Y'know, it just might work. I like it, Claudia! I like it a lot!"

Signorina Giorgi squeezed Mona's knee. "I knew you'd like it. This little scheme can't miss."

Claudia pulled up to the guard post at the Cinecittà lots and greeted the security man. "*Buono giorno*, Cesare! Listen, a friend of mine is coming by this morning in a 'fifty-one Fiat with a cracked windshield. Treat him nicely and show him the way to Theatre 14."

Cesare nodded and ogled Mona. Claudia drove on to the parking lot, passing a mocked-up frontier town for a spaghetti western and two spear-carriers from a Hercules saga.

"But what about Vincenzo?" Mona asked. "Is he hip to your big plan?"

Claudia pulled into her reserved parking space. "He will be. Don't say a word about it to anyone for now, especially Vincenzo. I plan to talk to him later today."

"How do you know he'll buy it?" Mona asked, lighting a menthol cigarette.

"Oh, he'll buy it, all right. You'll be giving him what he's always wanted—access to Hollywood. Besides boosting his career, it'll flatter his ego no end. And that's what really counts with Valentini."

The two women walked toward the doors of Theatre 14.

"There's just one unsolved question," Mona said. "How do we get out of our wedded bliss? A long marriage to Vincenzo doesn't fit in my plans."

"Don't worry. You'll be divorced in a year or so! In the interim, you don't even have to live together. Just show up at premieres and restaurants. Be seen at all the right places on both continents. The press will play you as the ultimate romantic couple. And the public will line up for blocks to see your movies."

Mona pinched her pixie pal's cheek as they walked onto the set of the *Inferno*. "You're a cagey little mover, Claudia. I'm glad I met you at the Limbo last night."

Claudia smiled sweetly. Everything was going as planned.

As the two women arrived, Theatre 14 was bustling with activity. The production crew had finished the assembly of the artist's studio from Giordano's dream. The set was replete with Persian carpets, filigree lamps, pillows, sofas, overstuffed chairs and curtained casements. Dolls, toy soldiers, a rocking horse, and street carousel littered the floor. An assistant director was positioning actors. There were models lounging in dishabille; a muscle man in posing trunks adoring himself in a mirror; a thin poet with a black cravat reading in a corner, and a pale woman with hair to her hips strumming a dulcimer.

In the middle sat Bartolomeo Cioffi, a grossly overweight actor recruited to play the painter. Vincenzo sat next to him looking fresh and rested for a change. He was wearing a light-weight beige suit.

Giordano Giorgi and Ettore were arguing over sketches of the castle exterior. Ettore pleaded and Giorgi fulminated. Claudia and Mona approached them with the press corps in tow.

"*Buon giorno, zio!* I've brought Mona Carlson to visit our little world!"

Giordano greeted Mona graciously but scowled at the pressmen. "What are these bastards doing here?" he demanded. "You know this set is closed to the press!"

Claudia spoke soothingly. "Uncle, the news guys can't resist Mona. They followed us here. When you think about it, it makes for great publicity. A few preview shots of Mona in front of the castle scene will really whet the public's appetite!"

"Damn their appetite!" fumed Giordano. "Let them feed on someone else's flesh!"

Mona waved and blew a kiss across the set to Vincenzo. "Oh, Mr. Giorgi," she cooed, as the grips and the camera men focused on her powder-blue presence, "everything looks so creative!"

While Giorgi zestfully traded insults with the journalists, Sandro Donati timidly walked in, squired by a studio page. Claudia directed her uncle away from the fracas to make introductions.

"Another special quest, *zio!* Giordano Giorgi, please meet Sandro Donati!"

Giorgi shook the young man's hand and looked at him piercingly. With his thick glasses, tweed jacket, and baggy pants Sandro made a scholarly, postgraduate impression. "Is he a critic?" Giorgi asked frankly.

"Uncle, this is the young actor I told you about. Sandro is a member of the Fontana Theatre Club. This season he's doing Ionesco, Arrabal, and Albee." Claudia gently removed Sandro's glasses. "See?"

Giorgi's eyebrows rose and again he peered at the young man intently. Others on the set looked over as well.

"Pretty kid," said Bartolomeo Cioffi.

"Almost like I was at his age," said Vincenzo.

Mona's eyes roamed over Sandro while she reflexively reached into her purse for a cigarette.

After a while Giordano Giorgi nodded. "*Sì, sì*, the camera will like him. We can use him as an extra in some of the scenes."

The paparazzi and reporters nosed in and started hurling questions.

"How far over budget are you?"

"Will Mona Carlson be appearing in the *Inferno*?"

GIORGI THREW HIS SKETCHPAD IN THE air. "This isn't a god-damned PR party! I'm trying to make a movie! With the exception of Miss Carlson, everyone not associated with this production will now leave the premises!"

The reporters yelped in protest.

"Young man," Giorgi said to Sandro, "Claudia will be in touch when we need you."

Security guards hustled the press out while Claudia walked Sandro to the door. "Don't worry," she said, in the sunshine outside Theatre 14, "you're in. And before the film's finished, you'll be a lot more than an extra!"

Sandro put on his glasses and looked pensive and skeptical. "I think you're a little crazy, *bambina*. Signor Giorgi will forget about me in five minutes."

Claudia took Sandro's face in her hand and kissed him good-bye. "You don't know Uncle. Your face is locked in his memory for good. Look, I've got lots more work to do today.

I'll see you sometime tomorrow. Then we'll talk about your part in the *Inferno*."

Back inside, Giorgi had retrieved his sketchpad and was squabbling with Ettore. Bartolomeo Cioffi and Renato Buonauito, the film's Virgil, were showering Mona with salacious compliments. Vincenzo was sitting by himself in a canvas chair, sipping mineral water.

Claudia took advantage of the moment and knelt down beside him. "Vincenzo!" she whispered, "I must meet with you tonight about a matter of the utmost importance."

Valentini chuckled. "You're not the first female to make that request."

"Listen, *buffo*," Claudia said, poking him in the shoulder, "I'm not kidding. I've got something very big to tell you. And it has to be absolutely secret!" She leaned in closer. "No dancing tonight. Mona will have to find another way to amuse herself. I'll meet you this evening alone, in your suite at the Excelsior."

Vincenzo was a little disturbed by her intensity. "Okay, okay! I'll meet you at the Excelsior at eight o'clock. You've got me wondering what this is all about."

"Absolute secrecy!"

Valentini relaxed and laughed softly. "Absolute secrecy, little sister. No one but you and I will know."

THAT EVENING CLAUDIA DRESSED EXPENSIVELY, BUT anonymously, for her visit to Vincenzo's hotel. She wore a simple gray suit with a modest matching hat and low black heels. Prim, non-prescription glasses completed her disguise—just another dull but wealthy tourist lady staying at the Excelsior.

She moved quickly through the lobby, avoiding the bank of elevators, and stepped quietly up the back staircase. She arrived at the top-floor landing, flushed and perspiring, then walked down the deep-piled hallway to the door of Vincenzo's suite. She tapped lightly at the door.

In a moment Vincenzo greeted her, dressed casually and holding a glass of scotch. He was genuinely surprised at her appearance. "Claudia Giorgi, is that you? The hippest, slickest babe in Rome dressed like a banker's wife?"

"Shhh, *buffo*! This is strictly confidential, remember?" Claudia stepped into the suite and closed the door behind her. "No one must know of this meeting!"

"I know, big secret," Vincenzo said cheerfully. "Can I offer you a drink?"

Claudia took in Valentini's richly appointed quarters. "Club soda with ice. *Grazie.*"

Valentini made the drink and handed it to her. "Now, what's this all about?"

"About you and Mona."

Vincenzo cocked his head. "Me and Mona? What's that to you?"

Claudia adjusted her incognito glasses. "Nothing and everything. You two are about to get married."

Vincenzo was initially silent, then burst out laughing and fell back on a velvet sofa.

Claudia stood with her arms crossed, glasses slipping down her nose. "*Si, buffo*, it's hilarious. I'm about to save your career and make you the world's biggest celebrity, and you think it's a joke!"

Vincenzo's disbelief subsided, as he propped his head up on a silk pillow. "Let me get this straight. I'm going to marry Mona Carlson. You're going to make me the world's biggest star." He mused for a moment then sprang to his feet. "You know what I think, Claudia? I think you're jealous of Mona! *Si*, don't laugh! You've been in love with me since you were a teenager, and this is the only way you can tell me. Hah! Don't give me that angry look! Why else would you be here, hot and bothered in your demure suit?!"

"Idiot! I'm flushed from climbing the damned stairs!" She gulped her club soda while Vincenzo stood with his hands on his hips.

"Si, little sister," he said. "You don't want Rome to know of our assignations, eh? You think Giordano would disapprove? Maybe. Who cares? You know, you look like a very sexy little banker's wife in that outfit."

Claudia realized she still had her dowdy hat on. She threw it off and pushed Vincenzo back. "I'm here for business, Signor Valentini, nothing else! If you'll just listen. . ."

With a sudden jump, Vincenzo grabbed Claudia and overwhelmed her with a passionate kiss. It was a move he'd made many times.

After what could be called a struggle, Claudia turned her face away and blocked Valentini's with her forearm. It was then that she experienced an uncharacteristic moment of confusion. She was in Vincenzo's hotel room on a well-defined mission. Of that she was sure. Vincenzo misconstrued her intent. That was obvious. On the other hand, she enjoyed the kiss, and with only one drink in him, Vincenzo was in control and very attractive. As they wrestled across the floor, she made a rapid-fire recalculation in her mind. A cold shower wasn't what was called for now. Valentini would be more easily compliant if his lust was satisfied. She'd relax for a few minutes and have some fun.

The wrestling intensified as she maneuvered Vincenzo into the bedroom.

"Claudia, Claudia, I must have you!" Vincenzo was very worked up.

Claudia resisted, strenuously, while kicking her shoes off and tearing Valentini's shirt open.

"Why do you fight me?!" he pleaded.

Claudia undid the buttons that Vincenzo fumbled with. Then with a little cry of feigned dismay, she pretended surrender in the grand style.

"*Mi amore!* Darling little Claudia. . ." Vincenzo groaned as they fell on satin sheets.

Vincenzo's slacks and Claudia's gray wool suit went flying. A battery of undergarments, stockings, and non-prescription glasses followed. They were intertwined and naked and all over each other very quickly.

To Claudia's delight, Vincenzo's performance was quite impressive. No signs of the flaccidity that had frustrated Mona. He was firm and sure and energetic in his attentions.

After more acrobatics, Claudia lay back and enjoyed her old fantasies of ravishment by her schoolgirl idol. She moaned and shuddered in counterpoint to Vincenzo's passionate thrusting. Then all came to a Vesuvian climax. Claudia swooned and Valentini made a heavy grunt.

Catching her breath, Claudia brushed her pixie bangs off her forehead. She stroked Valentini's back as he lay on her inertly. "Vincenzo, that was fantastic! The best!" she purred. "You're not so bad for an old man!" Vincenzo didn't return the postcoital banter. "Exhausted? Worn out from all that play?" She pinched his buttock.

Valentini didn't respond. His 154 pounds of flesh on top of her was beginning to feel more oppressive than cozy.

"Hey, Don Giovanni! Hey, *buffo*! After a good ride like that you go to sleep on me?"

Vincenzo didn't budge, grunt, or breathe.

"Jesus Christ, Vincenzo, wake up!"

With great effort, Claudia pushed up on her partner's shoulders until he slumped to the side of her. His face fell into a pillow and stayed there. Claudia squirmed up to a sitting position and shook Vincenzo with all her might. When he didn't react, she frantically felt for his pulse. No heartbeat. She rolled him over on his back and tried to revive him. She massaged, and then, pounded his chest, tried mouth-to-mouth resuscitation, then finally, desperately, ran to his bar, fetched a bucket, and threw ice water on his face.

No response.

"*Dio mio!*" Instinctively, Claudia reached for the bedroom phone to call for help. She stopped just as she was about to punch the button for the front desk. She put the phone down and sat naked on the bed next to Vincenzo Valentin's body.

She sat and thought very hard for a while, then got up and paced through the hotel suite. After five minutes, she came to a decision.

Vincenzo was gone, and nothing was going to bring him back. Calling the police or ambulance now would only result in scandal and colossal embarrassment. Vincenzo's dignity would be compromised. Her career at Cinecittà would be threatened. Even Uncle Giordano would be negatively impacted if the truth of the mess got out.

Claudia recovered her scattered clothes and dressed quickly. She put on her hat and non-prescription glasses. She washed her soda glass, being careful to remove her fingerprints, and put it back in the wet bar.

She gathered up Vincenzo's clothes, folded and hung them up neatly in the bedroom closet. She pulled a pair of dark blue pajamas out of a dresser and somehow got Vincenzo into them. She tidied up the bed and with great effort, changed the bottom sheet. She positioned the dead man in a supine position, pulled up the covers to his chest, and put a paperback book in his left hand. She put a half-glass of scotch on his bed-side table and turned the reading light on.

She combed Vincenzo's hair a bit and wiped any trace of her makeup off his face. She wiped the phone and went about the suite checking for any other signs of her visit. From all appearances, Vincenzo had died quietly, alone in his bed, while reading Mickey Spillane.

Claudia peeked out the suite's door and saw the hallway deserted. She left as she had come, utterly unnoticed.

When she arrived home at her apartment, she called the Excelsior and asked the front desk to ring Vincenzo's suite.

When she was told that there was no answer, she asked the clerk to send someone up to see if Signor Valentini was all right. She'd been expecting his phone call, she said, and was very concerned that she hadn't heard from him. The clerk told her to calm down, that he'd call her back as soon as someone had checked the room. Five minutes later Claudia let out a scream at her end of the phone as the clerk told her that Valentini was dead, apparently of a heart attack. The police and ambulance had been called.

Next morning production was shut down at Cinecittà. All the studios closed. Headlines in Rome's newspapers announced the shocking demise of "Italy's Beloved Screen Star—Dead of a Heart Attack, Age 43." Radio and TV buzzed with tributes and condolences. Many of those connected with the *Inferno* were interviewed. Critics instantaneously assessed Valentini's career and wrote glowing tributes. Obituaries appeared in the foreign press, and former costars and leading ladies wept in disbelief at his passing.

For his part, Giordano Giorgi went into hiding and refused to have anything to do with the press or anyone for days. Then one afternoon, about a week after Vincenzo's sudden demise, he asked Claudia to meet him at the Limbo. Its disconsolate manager, two gloomy waiters, and a bartender were the only staff in daytime. The only patrons were the director, his niece, and a few other refugees from the *Inferno*. With the band gone, the lights on, and the chairs up on most of the tables, the scene was appropriately bleak.

"After twenty years together, after all I went through with that bastard," Giordano cried, "he dies on me!"

Actually, he died on me, thought Claudia. She sniffled and wiped away a real tear.

"He would have achieved cinema immortality in the *Inferno*," said Giordano. "I know he struggled with the part, but he would have gotten it eventually. No more of the light comedy bullshit. They'd always remember his Dante."

"You can dedicate the film to his memory, *zio*," said Claudia, softly.

"What film?" snorted Giorgi. "There is no *Inferno* without Dante. The film's kaput!"

In the midst of mourning, Claudia was damned if she'd let opportunity slip away. "Sandro Donati, Uncle, Sandro Donati . . . ," she spoke his name like a mantra.

"The good-looking kid with the glasses?" The director's brow furrowed.

"He's a serious actor, *zio*. Like Brando, he's very skilled at improvisation. He's in love with the cinema. He's a natural star. And you see how beautiful . . ."

"But all wrong for the *Inferno*!" Giorgi said with finality. "Dante is a wasted man, a man who's looking back on life, trying to make some sense. He's wasted, he's gone astray. That's Vincenzo! God rest the bastard! He didn't have to act the part. He just had to stay sober and make his marks."

After all she'd been through, Claudia wasn't about to relent. "You can't give this film up, *zio*! You owe it to cinema history! Let the shock of Vincenzo's death wear off. Give it a little more time."

Renato Buonauito ambled glumly past them on his way to the men's room. Giordano watched him studiously. Then a little spark lit the director's baggy eyes. He gulped down his espresso, ordered another, lit a cigar, and lost himself in thought.

"I won't let you give up on the *Inferno*, *zio*. It would be like throwing away *Battleship Potemkin* or *Citizen Kane*!"

Giorgi flicked cigar ash. He spoke while looking into the middle distance. "You know, seeing Renato's sad ass drag by just now made me think of something." He flashed a dark little smile. "Maybe I've got the wrong writer guiding me. Maybe it's Virgil's poem I should be filming, not Dante's! *The Aeneid*! The young warrior who survives the sack of Troy and goes on many voyages. He beds down with Dido, queen of Carthage. But the gods have other plans for him! He sails to Italy, and after great battles, unites the Trojan and Latin peoples . . . !"

Claudia kept quiet and let him ramble.

"In effect, little niece, out of all his troubles, Aeneas creates the city of Rome!"

"I think I see where you're going," Claudia said, encouragingly.

"But *my* Aeneas will create *this* Rome! Modern Rome with all its lunacy! The gods let the mortals get out of hand and make something crazy!" The ideas were boiling up in him. He slapped his head. "Of course, now I see it, Claudia! Sandro Donati will be my young warrior who comes to modern Rome under the spell of the gods!"

Claudia gave a little squeal. She couldn't contain her sense of victory. She grabbed Giorgi's hand and squeezed it. She looked around Café Limbo in triumph. Then she saw a couple coming through the lattice of silk ivy.

As if conjured up by Giorgi's magic words, Sandro stood a few feet away, blinking. At his side was Mona Carlson.

Out of respect for Vincenzo's passing, Mona was all in black—a jet-black chemise dress that barely contained her, dark-tinted glasses, and stiletto heels. A little black hat was pinned to her tresses, and from it a mesh veil hung down over her eyes. "It's just terrible about Vincenzo." She sniffed.

"Italian cinema will never be the same without him. He was our Cary Grant." Sandro spoke to no one in particular. The world in front of him was a blur. His glasses were gone, along with his tweed jacket. He wore a crisp new blazer and an open-necked sports shirt. Tight dungarees replaced his baggy corduroys.

"Sandro and I are off to Spain this afternoon," said Mona, brightly. "He's going to be Nick Ray's new assistant! Isn't it wonderful!? We met at the Fontana Theatre Club, the night poor Vincenzo died. Isn't that something!"

"I can't believe it!" said Sandro, to the blurry shapes sitting at the café table. "Nicholas Ray! The great American auteur! The man who made *Johnny Guitar, They Drive by Night*, and *Rebel Without a Cause*!"

Claudia sat frozen in disbelief. Giorgi's eyes rolled heavenward as his mouth spouted volcanic cigar smoke.

Mona walked over to another table to say good-bye to Renato and Bartolomeo.

Claudia jumped up and strode over to her myopic boyfriend with fury in her eyes. "*Bastardo*!" she hissed. "Judas! I was going to make you a cine-star overnight! I went through hell for you, and now you're running off with this tart!"

With Claudia inches from his face, Sandro felt a sudden shock of recognition. "Claudia," he stammered, "you don't understand! Your uncle barely knows I exist. The most he'd ever give me is a bit part at best, and it would wind up on the cutting-room floor."

Claudia boiled. "You were going to be the star of the decade! Uncle was going to cast you as Aeneas in a new film!"

Sandro smiled indulgently and patted Claudia's shoulder. "You have a great imagination, *bambina*. But I've realized acting's not my life's work. Now I'll be behind the camera with Nicholas Ray, learning things from the inside, preparing to direct my own films."

Claudia threw her hands up and made a rude, noisy sound. She jabbed her finger in Sandro's chest. "And what's this with Mona, eh? You trade your little *bambina* for a barracuda, *porco*?"

Sandro drew himself up and tried to focus on Claudia's burning eyes. "Mona's a serious actress, and she's willing to help me. We've developed special feelings for each other!" he declared, defiantly.

"Special feelings!" Claudia shrieked. "*Buffo bastardo!* What about us, you silly son of a pig?!"

"Claudia," Sandro said, consolingly, "you and I can be friends. We can stay in touch. You're as sharp as they get, a great businesswoman. I'm sure I'll need your help one day!"

Claudia was hurt by Sandro's comments, but before she could reply, Pietro, the Limbo's owner, walked up to Sandro. "Back begging for a job, you bum? I told you last week you were through here. Get out or get thrown out!"

Sandro laughed in his face and a shouting match started. Annoyed by the racket, Giordano Giorgi rose to break up the fight.

Mona came over and pulled Claudia away. "Doesn't Sandro look gorgeous in that blazer I got him? And I threw away those dumb glasses of his. He can't see a damn thing, but he's got me to lead him," Mona giggled. She put her arm around Claudia's shoulder and walked the stunned publicist–casting director to a quiet corner. "When I saw him at Cinecittà, I *had* to have him. Whatever Mona wants. . . I heard you mention the theater club where he performs. I hunted him down!" Mona was cozy and confidential. Claudia listened in shock.

"He fell like a tonna bricks!" crowed Mona. "Although you know, he seems more interested in Nick Ray's stupid movies than my sex appeal! Anyway, he wasn't thinking about Nick when the lights were out."

Claudia looked at Carlson stonily.

"Hey, don't be pissed," said Mona. "I know you were working on getting him a part in the *Inferno*. But that's small-time stuff. You got more important things to think about than finding bit players for your uncle. You're one smart cookie!" She gave Claudia's cheek a pinch. "Anyway, I'm getting Sandro a gig as a gofer in Nick's movie. You know, he'll get coffee, run to the lunch wagon for sandwiches, that kind of thing. Strictly nonunion!" Mona rolled her eyes. "His real job will be keeping Mona happy. And believe me, he's got the equipment for it!"

Mona giggled and poked Claudia's ribs. She turned to look at Sandro who was standing alone, gazing lamely at the blurry café. Giorgi and Pietro were walking away from him, trading sentimental stories about Vincenzo.

"Listen, Claudia, we got a plane to catch. I'm sorry things didn't work out like you and I planned, and I'm really sorry about Vincenzo. But hey! He had a good life!" Mona winked. "Oh well, I got a nice toy to play with, thanks to you. You take care. You got a great future in the business. Maybe we'll meet again."

Mona gave Claudia an affectionate hug. Then she turned and click-clacked across the floor to her half-blind companion. She slithered around Sandro like a python and wriggled the pair out of Café Limbo like one four-legged, two-headed creature.

Looking shell-shocked and forlorn, Claudia took a seat by a fake palm. Giordano Giorgi walked up to his niece. "Looks like Aeneas is off to Carthage with Dido. Don't worry, *bambina*. Rome is lousy with starving actors waiting to be discovered. Back when the dinosaurs roamed, I used to be one."

"*Si, zio*," Claudia said, cheerlessly.

"I'll see you later," said Giordano. "I'm going out to Cinecittà."

Claudia looked up at him. "The studios are still closed."

"I know. All the better. I want to be alone with Valentini's ghost. I still have a few things to say to that bastard."

Claudia cracked a facsimile of a smile.

"You know," continued Giorgi, "I sometimes go to Cinecittà on Sundays and sit by myself chatting with cinema's ghosts. The cleaning ladies think I'm crazy."

"The cleaning ladies are right, *zio*. Go on, go commune with your spirits. *Ciao*."

Giorgi gave his niece a hug then strode out of the Limbo, sans entourage.

Claudia sat alone by the palm tree, one hot tear running down her cheek. Reflecting bitterly, she saw her master plan in ruins. Her fast-forward motion derailed. "*Buffa*," she said out loud to herself. "Little fool!" All her efforts had come to nothing. She'd let two pathetic men and a tart do her in!

Of course, Uncle would be all right. After conversation with the film phantoms and a few more blue days remembering Vincenzo, he'd regain his insatiable appetite for life and start up again. Dreams would pour out of his head and find their fated place on celluloid. And, of course, until it was time for her to do something else, she'd write copy for the press to play with and talk up the production. Whether it was the *Inferno*, the *Aeneid*, or something out of the comic strips, it really didn't matter. All of it was Giordano Giorgi's ongoing poem of himself.

As for Vincenzo, she angrily anticipated being haunted by his vain, smug shade. Together they made the great black joke that could never be told: The great Don Giovanni dies in the saddle, riding a spirited little filly! Just her luck to keep secret the most sensational story of all. Certain headlines were condemned to a lifetime's concealment in her mind: "PR Girl's Passion Slays Screen Idol!" "Mystery Woman Seen Leaving Star's Hotel Suite!" "Comely Claudia—Valentini's Last Stand!"

Claudia stood up so quickly her head bumped a palm frond. She looked daggers at the plant and smoothed her ruffled hair. It was time to go, time to jump in the Alfa and drive. Drive out of the lunatic city, away from the film business, into the countryside, where there were flowers and sky! She'd drive like lightning.

Claudia exited the Limbo and had her keys out of her shoulder bag half a block before reaching the Alfa. She slid down into the driver's seat and kicked off her shoes. She switched on the ignition, got into gear, and let her bare feet floor the foot pedals. Then she gunned the motor and roared into midday traffic with the radio blasting. She shot down the Via Veneto with a vengeance, into the dense mist of car fumes. She was fed up with everything, driving like the wind. Had her uncle been there to see her, he would have seen his vision of a modern Roman goddess, racing her chariot through the clouds.

# Ursula and the Sublime

THE LIFE OF URSULA CAMPION, THE Romantic-era painter who produced a major body of work in a hailstorm of exuberant creativity, has been elaborated in numerous biographies. James Cross, the first to publish an account of Campion's life, made bare mention of her paintings and based his telling on lurid speculations of her personal life. Written within months of the discovery of Campion's battered corpse in the ruins of the Coliseum in February 1824, Cross's depiction remained the "life" of the artist most people envisioned until the turn of the century. At that time, Campion's work, known for its notoriety rather than invention during her lifetime, finally began to receive the serious attention it deserved. Following critical praise, Cross' prurient fable was finally corrected by a series of critical biographies, most notably those of Milton Skelton, Rosetta Cornwall and Lawson Owen. Then in 1952, the exhaustively researched *Ursula Campion: Mistress of the Sublime* by Vivian Gwent became the "authoritative life."

Soon to add to the fascination Campion still holds on our imaginations will be *The Diaries of Ursula Campion (1820–1824)*, forthcoming next month from Morgan and Dent. Begun as a trip book on a tour of the Lake District and northern Wales, Lawson Owen was the first to mention the diaries, yet even by the time of Gwent's study, their existence remained a mystery. Fortunately, that changed two years ago when workers renovating the Caffé Greco near the Spanish Steps discovered eight ribbon-bound journals in a stuffy cabinet in one of the café's old, elegant rooms.

The following is a selection from the two-volume *Diaries of Ursula Campion (1820–1824)*, edited and with an introduction by Vivian Gwent. The selection begins with an excerpt recorded shortly after the opening of *Views of Snowdon and Wales*, the exhibit that brought celebrity to Campion at the age of twenty-three.

*1820*
*30 December*
I'm working now from sketches I made in the Lake District. There's so much material to draw from—sketches in pencil, watercolours, a few quick sketches in oil. It seems like ages ago that I made the trip. I'd nearly forgotten how much that wild, uncultivated landscape inspired me. The tour lasted only three weeks, but I have enough material to keep me busy for months. I have great views of the most spectacular locations—Windemere and Derwentwater, Keswick, Scale Force, and the towering peak of Scafell Pike. I'm going to create enough paintings for a new exhibition, paintings that will surpass in sheer size and affect the work in *Views of Snowdon and Wales*. That work I now regard as utterly tame and picturesque.

*1821*
*18 February*
Alfred Gye has now twice been to the studio. When he left this afternoon we made a tentative date for

another visit. Dare I flatter myself that it's more than my paintings he's interested in? He'll make a slightly favourable comment about a landscape and then tell me that my paintings are unnecessarily large. I'll feel his critical eyes moving from the canvas to my ankles, my hair, and my breasts. What a marvelous tension is brewing. Although we do nothing more than reenact our roles from the Academy—he the somewhat aloof dispenser of knowledge, me the humble gatherer of the crumbs he dispenses—there's an excitement bred of the fact that we're no longer student and teacher. Today, before he left, he brushed against me. I felt a charge through my body and turned a brilliant virginal pink. What will become of it? He's being so solicitous!

*26 March*

Father is furious about me staying overnight in the studio. I think his fury is a lot of bluster and merely masks his concern. He knows nothing of the affair with Alfred Gye. If he did, he'd cancel the lease on the studio. He worries about the high profile that *Views of Snowdon and Wales* has brought me and about my being alone in a building of single flats in New Bond Street. Poor Father. There is nothing I can do, shy of a conventional marriage, to bring him peace of mind.

*21 April*

I've been struggling now for weeks with my painting of Scale Force. The task is monumental and involves nothing less than my reeducation as a painter. How to free myself from technical restraints and make the painting ring with spontaneity? How to eliminate detail and still suggest boundlessness? How to make

the viewer feel the remarkable power of the Scale—
the fear I felt when standing on the dangerous out-
cropping, the water cascading down from the high
crags, the mist blowing in my face? How to make the
viewer hear the terrifying roar of the waterfall? I've
had some success working in watercolour on very large
pieces of paper. Limiting the palette to greys and blue
greens has helped to create a mood of brooding
tumult. And by using small dense strokes and broad
washes, I've been able to alternately convey mass and
space. But I'm still so far from my ultimate goal. Such
a painful discrepancy exists between what I saw and
felt at Scale Force and what I've been able to reproduce with pigment and paper. I'm hopeful that when
the painting is translated into oil on canvas, three
times the size of the paper I've been using, it will have
the desired effect.

*11 May*

From original pencil sketches, to watercolour sketches,
to sketches in oil, to oil on canvas—finally, with
*Derwentwater: Rainbow* I'm beginning to paint the
kind of painting I've wanted to paint. It could be
larger, but at 1m x 1.25m, it's my largest to date. It's
my first painting in which scale, mass, and space are
conveyed entirely through light, colour, and brush-
strokes. For the first time, there are no sheep in the
foreground, no shepherds or trees to establish propor-
tion. I've done away with all that! I've also done away
with my timid palette! *Derwentwater: Rainbow* has a
full range of colour to express a full range of emotion!
It captures the exhilaration of that solitary moment
when the dark clouds parted after a storm. A shaft of
light poured down through the opening in the clouds

and a brilliant rainbow arch appeared over the lake. It was absolutely spellbinding. I felt as though the arch had been put there, purposely, to put an end to my growing doubts about providence.

*12 June*
I don't know how much more of my exile in Kensington I can stand. At times, I think I might go mad—mad from routine and boredom. Though I must say, the interminable quiet and lack of any activity have been a balm to body and soul. After Alfred and the completion of *Derwentwater: Rainbow*, I felt utterly depleted and invaded with darkness. I'd never known such despondency before. For days I sat and looked at the studio walls. I couldn't work. I didn't want to wash or dress myself. Clarissa knew something was wrong when after a week she hadn't received a single letter. For sisters who write each other daily it was unprecedented. So, Father was alerted. He came and fetched me from New Bond St., and I've been in Kensington ever since. Initially, the comfort of my old room and the constant pampering felt good. However, now my restlessness is resurfacing with a vengeance.

*20 July*
How I envy Clarissa's composure. She's the compliant daughter I could never be. Yesterday we opened my specimen box from the Lake District. Clarissa's kept it at her bedside since I first gave it to her. She moved her delicate fingers over the samples of moss, rock, and dried flowers. She told me that she often gazes into the box and imagines herself accompanying me in the Lakes. She's quite content with that daydream,

whereas I could never be satisfied with mere imaginings. Could two sisters be of more contrary spirit, or any closer? During my recuperation, we've exchanged the most intimate thoughts. I told her about my affair with A. As awful as it was, I have no regrets. After all, we are forces of nature—more than the beasts, but not quite angels. I told Clarissa I want to pursue every adventure that comes my way, every experience, as long as it's not superficial! She said I must! For her as well as for myself, I must seek every sensation and indulge every desire. I'm more robust, so I must do it for the both of us. At night, by candlelight, she read me drafts from her first novel, tentatively titled *Bella of the Moors*. Such poignant insight! Such lucid observation! Such passion! Where does it come from? Her exterior is so deceptive; she seems to hang to life by a thread, yet within the confines of this house, the confines of her fancy, she can experience all of human nature. Truly, it's a marvel. I told her it had to be published, and I would use what contacts I have to see that it is. She's agreed, as long as we employ her pen name, Charlotte Waite! Yet another secret to keep from Father!

*15 November*

The most exquisite creature came to the party last night. The most beautiful, fragile-looking man. The sight of him was as arresting as my first sight of the shaft of light at Derwentwater. The way he moved around the studio, like a wounded god or a wounded angel. He seemed to beg for my protection. His name is Robert Harlow and he's a pianist. Henry Bentham invited him to the party, or rather a friend of a friend of Henry's invited him. Everyone here last night was a friend, or a friend of my former Academy classmate—mostly literati, as Henry's current infatuation is a poet, a very bad one, who Henry says is endowed with physical attributes which more than compensate for his lack of prowess with the pen. Henry had just installed a piano (I suppose to impress his poet), but as neither he nor I play very well, a pianist was called for. Thus Robert Harlow! O! The thought of him playing—absorbed in ecstatic contemplation—his long fingers gliding over the keys, his pained eyes looking up to the ceiling whenever the music gained in intensity. I could abandon myself to him, totally.

*1822*
*24 May*
This afternoon by the pond, I rested my head on Robert's lap. He read to me from Longinus, *On the Sublime*. "Lifting up the soul and exalting it to ecstasy. . . allowing the soul to participate in the splendors of divinity." The words describe the effect of the sublime on our souls when we come upon it in poetry; they could just as easily be describing the power of certain scenes in the Lakes, or the magnetic attraction that spontaneously erupts between one person and another. Sublimity is anything that makes the soul multiply, expand and reverberate without end. How ironic that the words should be read in the formal gardens at Northcote. Here all of nature has been conquered and tamed by Father's gardener. It's not at all inspiring. Robert says that things are only as sublime as the mind that perceives them. I disagree. Certain places and people compel us with their sublimity.

*5 August*

Mozart, Mozart, Mozart! Our Northcote idyll is proving to be tremendously productive for both of us. Robert's decided to give a recital when we return to London in October. Until then I expect to hear nothing but Mozart. I've helped him make a selection of my favorite sonatas and concertos. It's a joy to see him this productive, but his long, torturous hours of practice drive me mad. Fortunately, I can escape to my studio. It's in the ballroom, in a separate wing of the house. I'm working on my first mural-sized painting, a view of Keswick. The enormous size of the ballroom allows me the freedom to work on this scale. It's truly exhilarating, though I'm making a mess of this gorgeous room. Father will rant and rave, but he shouldn't expect me to sit in the garden and paint pretty pictures while I'm here.

*27 August*

I believe *Scale Force* will have to be my last view of the Lake District. With its completion, I've exhausted the subject. More than thirty paintings, three of them mural size. There's enough for a second exhibition and some much-needed sales. I'm down to the last few pounds of my annuity, most of which has been allocated to Robert's laudanum. If I can sell some paintings, I can take him away to Switzerland. He's in such a terrible way. The stress of his upcoming recital has been devastating to his health. He's absolutely ashen and has become so thin. When he coughs, his handkerchief is saturated with blood. Only Clarissa knows. If Father knew, he'd have a fit! Father knows nothing of Robert and hasn't the slightest inkling that I've had him here at Northcote. Thank god!—Father rarely visits Northcote at this time of year. I don't know what would happen if he walked in on us. Most likely he'd have Robert deported to the nearest asylum and drag me back to London. I can't stand it! It's all I can do to maintain a cheerful facade, to nurse him. I try to see that he gets some tea and broth, daily. Unfortunately, laudanum has become his only comfort, the only thing that will induce sleep. I look about the house. It's a metaphor for our malaise. The velvet cloth on the piano hasn't been raised in days—with the recital scheduled for two weeks from today! And my studio! I've never neglected it like this. It's a mess! Paints, brushes, and rags strewn all over. I try to keep things clean, to avoid the buildup of dust and overwhelming odors, but I've been distracted—and Robert's cough worsens.

*28 September*

Henry Bentham and I crossed the Pass of St. Gothard today, following the river down towards the Italian lakes. Travel is not Henry's forte. He complains constantly of the narrowness of the roads and the sheerness of the cliffs dropping down beside them. Can't he see the rapturous beauty of it all? I'm seduced by the shadowy chasms. Peering down into the depths arouses a thrilling sensation in me. At Devil's Bridge this morning, I filled half a notebook with pencil sketches. There are high emerald meadows everywhere! I gather specimens of rocks and wild flowers. When we return to England, I'll place them on Robert's grave.

*9 October*

Spent the entire day in the coach, twisting and winding along the steep cliffs. I saw a magnificent glacier turn from pale rose to gold in the early morning light. At Faido, a small rock fall made our horses lose their footing. Our left rear wheel went spinning off the road. For what seemed like an eternity, we hung over the massive rocks and vehement river far below. It was terrifying—especially when I craned my neck out the window to look down into the abyss. The coach rocked back and forth. Henry let out a blood-curdling scream. He turned white as a shade and nearly fainted when our driver told us that a postchaise had fallen into the ravine three days before killing the coachman and all three passengers. Once righted and on our way, a storm came on. Thunder and lightning of staggering force. I could hear Robert telling me that it was my mind that was making the storm sublime. This evening when we reached the Cistercian convent, Henry went to bed without supper and I dined alone. Afterwards, I stepped out into the cold darkness. The night was filled with the sound of eerie, distant cowbells and the stars were so close, I could feel their heat penetrating my coat and dress. I reached out to the star that was nearest and brightest. I'm sure Robert was there.

*31 October*

We're resting in a villa on Lake Lugano. I've rented it for a month before resuming our journey. God knows! The Alps were so harrowing, we need the rest. Henry is his old self in luxury's lap. He's wasted little time acquainting himself with the local aristocracy. Claudio, Henry's newest and dearest friend, is the son of a nobleman from Castagnola. Claudio comes to the villa every night. A rather dull boy, but he is resourceful. He's introduced us to the pleasures of hashish—hashish and red Italian wine. The hashish is remarkable. It allows me to recall so vividly all the spectacular sights we came upon in the Alps. The effect doesn't last long, but while I'm under the influence, I'm content to dwell on my visions, in a cocoon of divine concentration. At those moments I have no desire to share what I'm experiencing with Henry or Claudio. Until it wears off and the wine loosens my tongue, I'm silent. I never tried Robert's tinctures of opium and brandy, but having experienced hashish and wine every day, I can appreciate the relief the laudanum must have brought him towards the end.

*1823*

*23 January*

Henry has joined the Roman community of British expatriates. I'm amazed at how large and active a community it is. They have parties every night. I went to a few before I became sickened with boredom. It's far more exciting to stay home and paint! I've completed three dozen watercolours and two large oils since we arrived. I think I'm breaking new ground—especially when I look at the last oil, *Mountain Road at Faido*. I wonder if it didn't have a title, would anyone have any idea as to what the subject is? Even the line of the horizon, which would ordinarily guide the eye into the landscape, is obscured. I no longer think perspective is particularly important. It's not important that the viewer see, in any conventional sense, the road, the peaks, the crashing river over the rocks, the chasm far below. It's more important that the viewer feels the emotional charge of the atmosphere— the real threat of danger at that moment. There are so many densely hatched strokes in *Mountain Road at Faido*, going in so many directions; the viewer may well experience vertigo! For the first time since Robert's death, I'm excited with work. I can feel his hand holding mine, guiding the brush.

*14 July*

Six months of frantic activity, an uninterrupted surge of energy, and now nothing. Even if I wanted to add to the alpine series, I couldn't. I've exhausted myself with the huge, almost monochromatic *Mer de Glace*. I challenge anyone, upon viewing it, not to feel as though they've stepped into a vast outdoor cathedral at the moment of creation. It's an enormous abstraction of light and colour, predominated by broad washes. It's a great personal achievement, but its cost has been great. I feel the way I felt after the completion of *Derwentwater: Rainbow.* Everything is dark. My interior's dark. I draw all the shades to block out the Roman sun. I feel so empty and think of ending it all and joining Robert. I'm frightened when this mood overcomes me. To steady my nerves, I've been relying on laudanum. I'd give anything for Clarrisa to join me. She alone could restore calm—but the poor dear hasn't the stamina to make the journey. Every day Henry urges me to explore the glories of Rome with him, to get out and meet people. That's the tonic, he says. Clarissa encourages me to take his advice. But what glories are there? Cities are uninspiring. I've yet to meet a soul who interests me.

*10 August*

Last night, after days of inactivity, I let Henry talk me into accompanying him to the Prince's *Ball for the Liberation of Halicon.* It was quite the scene, hundreds of elaborately dressed Europeans, Americans and wealthy Romans swirling around the dance floor. The heat was stifling and I could barely tolerate the crowd. I was ready to leave when Henry grabbed me by the waist and pushed me onto the receiving line. There was the Prince, nodding his head, smiling and taking the hand of everyone presented to him. When it came my turn, he took my hand and wouldn't release it. His eyes fixed on mine. They held danger, risk, and excitement. Prince Isidore Cosim-Voloshin—the first truly compelling man I've met since our arrival in Rome. He's Russian, a Count, who makes his home here. There are all sorts of rumors about him. He's said to have one of the largest collections of Renaissance paintings in Italy, to have murdered a prostitute, and to be financing the revolution in Greece. He's marvelous to look at, big and dark—the complete opposite of Robert.

*1 October*
Weightlessness and painlessness, that's what the opium brings. Without it I wouldn't be able to recover from these long nights with Isidore. He has an enormous appetite for unconventional activity in the boudoir. After the compromised nature of my sexual relations with Robert, being with Isidore is like being with a volcano. When we've spent ourselves, the opium brings dreams of Robert. They're not at all the nightmares I had feared. They're intensely comforting dreams. When I wake from them, I feel as though Robert has actually visited me, and the piercing emptiness I've felt since his death passes away.

*1824*
*9 February*
I've been having Isidore's coachman make detours to the Coliseum on the way to the palazzo at night. They

say it's dangerous, even in the day. Camps of thieves and gypsies make it their homes there and prey on the tourists—but the haunting darkness of the ancient ruin has captured my imagination. I've finally found something architectural that excites me. I want to fill notebooks with nightpieces of the strange shadows cast by the arches in the moonlight. I foresee a whole series on the Coliseum to follow the alpine series. Thus far I haven't had any trouble while I'm sketching. No one has approached me or threatened me. My biggest fright came when a stray cat darted across my path. I know that should I ever feel frightened, the coachman is waiting outside to take me to Isidore— my dark angel. What a strange twilight world he's introduced me to. I rise now after noon. Then the coachman brings me back to the house I still share with Henry, though I rarely see him. I rarely eat. I've started making an oil from one of the night sketches from the Coliseum. With landscapes I wanted to obliterate the vistas. Now I want to obliterate the ancient ruins, or just hint at them. I'm using the darkest palette I've ever used—greys, lavenders, umber, black. The colours aren't all that dissimilar from the hair and eyes of the woman in my mirror. My former vibrancy must have been exhaled through the opium pipe. My chestnut curls haven't been washed in days. I'm pale and thin, with dark circles under my eyes, the colour drained from my lips—but for my hair colour, I'm like a female version of Robert towards his end. I wake, come home, paint, smoke my pipe, and wait for Isidore's coachman to return.

# Blue Corpus Christi

IT WAS THE MONDAY FOLLOWING THE feast of Corpus Christi. We'd just laid Eduardo's companion to rest. My overnight train to Madrid was due in two hours, and we were waiting out the time on the terrace of the Café Belmonte.

"Are you thinking of coming to Madrid, Eduardo? It's wonderful. The galleries, all the latest art and poetry, the best jazz, the latest films from Hollywood."

My brother was gulping brandy from a flask and staring at the river.

"Eduardo?"

He didn't answer but let his eyes scan the carnival vans boarded up on the banks of the Guadalquivir.

"Body of Christ," he finally said. "Bloody body of Christ. When the priest raised the host I saw Paco inside the closed coffin. Paco in a stiff black suit and starched white shirt. So pale. So delicate. His fine bones and translucent skin. His hands folded on his chest with their prominent blue veins."

Above us the sky was a cloudless, blazing field of blue. The blue as I imagined it in Lorca's poem about the holidays.

> *. . . gliding by.*
> *The carousel brings them*
> *and takes them away.*
>
> *Blue Corpus Christi,*
> *White Christmas Eve.*

I REMEMBERED LORCA READING THE LINES to me a year ago as a sympathetic gesture from one homesick Andalusian to another.

"Won't you at least consider spending the summer with me? My apartment is huge. Madrid is just the change you need. All the excitement. The freedom. I'll introduce you to my theater friends, everyone in La Barraca. I'll introduce you to García Lorca. You can join the troupe. Think of it. Taking Lope de Vega and Calderón to the provinces. I know you wouldn't want to act, but there are plenty of other things you could do. Painting and constructing sets, designing posters, writing press releases. Or, if you prefer, you could just stay in Madrid. Think of the opportunities to pursue your poetry."

"A red rose from a climbing vine. I managed to find one and place it beside him in the coffin."

Poor Eduardo. He was by nature a serious person. Serious about everything—poetry, politics, love. But Paco's death had weighted his seriousness with remorse. It was difficult to see him so distressed, to see him drinking so much. I thought if I could lure him into the light of my adopted city, he'd have a chance to come out of the shadows.

He took another sip of brandy. "In the coffin I saw the boy again, the boy I held in my arms in the thunderstorm. In his grandfather's fields we walked through rows of olive trees into a clearing. It was four in the afternoon. The sky darkened. A strong wind came out of nowhere. Paco was some distance from me when lightning struck the ground close to where he was standing. I ran to him. His face was white. He told me his chest was burning, that he'd been brushed by the fingers of God. Like a child he was. A boy of sixteen with wonder and terror on his face. I drew him near me to calm him. His shirt was open. There was a red blush over his heart."

"You never told me that story," I said, wondering when Belmonte would ever come and take our order. I wanted to make sure Eduardo ate something before it was time to leave for the station.

"It was this time of year, several years ago, though it feels like yesterday. It was the beginning of summer, Corpus Christi time. I'd just finished my first year of university in Seville. The family was still here in Mendoza, before Father moved us to Cordoba. You, Angelina, were a little convent schoolgirl."

I had to laugh. "Oh, God, those days. The Mother Superior who fancied herself another Teresa of Ávila. She actually told us that if we had eyes to see, we'd glimpse the Holy Spirit on her shoulder and our own shoulders, as well."

My brother ignored my recollection. "The day following the thunderstorm I watched the Corpus Christi procession from our balcony. I knew Paco would be in it. I was waiting for him. When he appeared, he looked so proud in his Moorish dress, riding high in the saddle. He glanced up at me with eyes that offered everything I'd ever wanted."

Eduardo fingered his flask. "He was so out of place on his grandfather's ranch with his father, his uncles, his brothers. They were rough *ganaderos*, used to breeding the bulls. He wasn't the boy for that life.

"That summer, my first summer with Paco, you, Mother, and Father went to Cordoba to visit Aunt Concha. Paco and I had the house to ourselves. We spent hours on the rooftop playing our game of Saint Sebastian. What a beautiful Sebastian he made with his white skin and a linen sheet around his hips. I was Diocletian, condemning him to death. In place of arrows I placed rose thorns on his chest, belly, and thighs. Paco would groan in his martyrdom. Then Diocletian would exit. I'd return as the pious widow who found the saint and nursed him back to health. One by one, I removed the thorns. I unwrapped the sheet and washed his limp body."

The brandy had loosened my brother's reserve. I was pleased that he was opening up, but I knew the nature of his memories were inappropriate for a café in our childhood home. I didn't want him to be overheard. "Eduardo, keep your voice down."

"Why? We're the only ones here."

JUST THEN BELMONTE CAME OUT AND started taking the chairs down from the other tables. He looked like he always had. Short and solid. His skin dark and wrinkled. He smiled at me the way he used to smile when I was a girl in town with her family, shopping or attending a festival. He came over when I signaled.

"I know we're your first customers, but our request is a simple one. We'd like bread and cheese and two café solos."

"*Sí*, Señorita Flores."

"And some of the Corpus Christi Carmelite crescents."

"Señorita is too late, they're all gone. But there are other sweets."

"No. I had a craving for the little yellow crescents. I think of them when I think of the festival."

"You must come back next year just for the festival, Señorita. Then you'll have all the yellow crescents you like."

"I'd like that. I'd like to return in happier times and stay longer than two nights."

Belmonte gave Eduardo a stern look then looked back at me. "*Sí*, Señorita. It's for the funeral of young Señor Camacho that you and your brother have come back to Mendoza." I thought I detected a hint of disgust at the mention of Paco's family name. "It's very sad that your brother has had to bury his friend. My condolences, Señor Flores," he said in a patronizing tone.

Eduardo stiffened but ignored Belmonte's comment and stared at the river.

"I'm afraid my brother's thoughts are elsewhere. You'll have to excuse him. It's been an unexpected loss. I'm trying to convince him to give up his teaching post in Seville and join me in Madrid. It would be a good change."

Belmonte frowned. "Perhaps it's not my business, Señorita, but I've known you all your life. I think it's better that you live in Mendoza or Cordoba than Madrid. Madrid is not a good place for a young, well-bred lady."

"Señor Belmonte, I'm a grown woman. I don't want to leave Madrid. What troubles you about it?"

"The people, the government. They're hurting the country, destroying our traditions."

Eduardo continued to ignore Belmonte, but his flushed face told me he was riled by what he heard.

"In Madrid they're turning everything upside down. Everything that makes Spain great, they wish to do away with. They defame the church. They put false ideas in the minds of the schoolchildren. They're ruining the economy. They call day night and night day." He looked again at Eduardo. "The men there behave as women, and the women behave as men."

"Do you think I behave as a man?"

Belmonte threw up his hands. "Of course I don't refer to the señorita. You're a gracious lady from an honorable family. It's best that you return to Mendoza and leave Madrid to the Communists."

I laughed at Belmonte, while Eduardo went rigid with anger. "I'm sorry you don't care for Madrid, Señor Belmonte. I like our capital very much. As for the new government, they look to the future. They want a modern Spain."

Belmonte gave a deferential nod. "As you please, Señorita. I find the old ways best."

"I like some of the old ways, as well. I adore the pageantry of the holidays, the Carmelite sweets, many things, but Spain can't stay in the past forever. It's time to give up the things that hold us back. It's time to catch up with the rest of Europe."

Belmonte shrugged. "Your new ways, your modern ways, what good did they do for Señor Camacho?" Again, I heard disapproval when the Camacho name passed through his lips. He didn't wait for an answer, but went inside the café.

When he was out of sight Eduardo spoke. "That little Fascist! I can't stand for the name Camacho to pass through his lips. I ought to punch his face!" My brother's bloodshot glare contrasted sharply with the elegance of his dark blue suit and the small, perfect rose in his lapel.

"Lower your voice! He's just a simple old man."

"He's a member of the local Falange! He'd cut our throats if he was told to."

"Please, someone will hear you!" I found Eduardo's accusation about the Falange hard to believe, but my brother wasn't given to unfounded speculation. "Mendoza's a small Andalusian town filled with country people. Country people with country ideas and country expectations. You're imposing your politics on these simple, uncomplicated people."

"These simple, uncomplicated people killed Paco!"

"Paco died of a ruptured spleen. You're really getting drunk, *hermano*."

"I'm not drunk," Eduardo said, in an attempt at a whisper. "Paco was murdered by your simple country people."

"How do you know?"

"He told me before he died."

"What did he tell you?"

"He told me he'd come home for the holiday with forebodings. He hadn't been in touch with his family for months. He said. . ."

Eduardo went silent at Belmonte's approach. The old man set down a basket of rolls, Manchegan cheese, and two black coffees. He bowed politely and went back inside the café.

Eduardo drained the last of his brandy and resumed. "His family hated him for what he'd become, for what he always was, really. His leaving home for the streets of Seville put an end to their pathetic hopes for their youngest son. Paco's mother blamed me, of course. She only let me see him in the end because he demanded it. He was dying. They called me on Wednesday. The priest had just performed the last rites when I arrived."

"What did Paco tell you?"

"As was customary, he'd come home for the holiday to see family and join his brothers in overseeing the estate. It was a formality. He was inept at outdoor work. His brothers treated him with contempt, all but Luis, the only one who wasn't a brute.

"Saturday night, a week ago, they played cards with the ranch hands. Everyone got drunk and boisterous. One of the ranchers tried to kiss Paco. He called him a *maricón*. Luis stepped up and punched the guy. A fight broke out. Arms and fists flailing. During the brawl, Paco was kicked over and over in the torso. Luis tried to stop it, but his other brothers held him back.

"When the fighting was over, Paco stumbled back to the main house with Luis's help. In his bedroom he vomited blood. Less than a week later he was dead."

"Did they try to save him?"

"Old Dr. Ribera was summoned a few days after the fight. By then it was too late. The spleen had ruptured. He had peritonitis. He was slipping away in delirium. Evidently, the only time he was lucid was during his last moments with me."

"Did they arrest the men who kicked him?"

"Two ranch hands were let go. But the general opinion of Paco's family was that it was an unfortunate accident."

"It's a terrible thing that's happened, Eduardo. I mean the men getting drunk and fighting. That's what they do. It's just hard to believe his brothers would hold Luis back while Paco was being kicked. It's also hard to believe the men involved intended to kill Paco."

"Oh, you're wrong, *hermana*. It was intentional! The swine that kicked him knew they had the endorsement of Paco's family. They knew what the family thought of him. He wasn't just a disgrace. He was a freak, a mutant, something to be eradicated, erased, forgotten. The swine knew there would be no repercussions! If anything, there'd be a reward. We're talking about a murder of opportunity."

EDUARDO'S GRIM STORY WAS INTERRUPTED BY two honks from a gleaming yellow roadster pulling up outside the café. Enrique Ruiz-Escribano, our host in Mendoza, had come to drive me to the railroad station.

Enrique eased his enormous body out of the car and climbed the steps to the café. A white linen suit draped his tall corpulence, making his progress around the people now gathering on the patio like that of a graceful white elephant moving among gazelles.

"Ah, my little flower," he said, taking my hand, "sorry to have kept you waiting. I hope your petals haven't begun to wilt."

"You're timing is just right," I said, forcing a smile in the midst of Eduardo's gloom.

Enrique fit himself into the chair beside me. "I would have come back sooner, but Mother had a million things she wanted me to pick up. Since I dropped you off, I've been to five shops." He brushed his long, straight hair away from his round face.

"Such a dutiful son," I said.

"I knew you'd understand, my angel. This dress is gorgeous," he said, stroking my sleeve. "Pink peonies on a black background. And the black straw cloche. Perfect! Even in mourning you manage to be glamorous." He shot a look at my silent, brooding brother. "I see someone's in a brown study."

"Do you believe this fabric?" I said, trying to keep the conversation light. "Madrid is fantastic. I don't have to wait years to see the Paris fashions."

"I'm so glad you've put the peasants and gypsies of Andalusia behind you. Moving to Madrid is the best thing you could have done. You're getting a chance to fulfill your destiny," he said, stealing another glance at a self-absorbed Eduardo. "To think I've had the leading actress of Lorca's La Barraca as a houseguest!"

"I'm hardly the leading actress, but thank you. I had a part in *Blood Wedding*, and I play the second female lead in our production of Calderón."

"Well, if you're not the leading actress now, you will be soon. I hear Hollywood beckoning."

"Oh please . . . just as long as I remain your little Angelina, the one you've been teasing for twenty-two years."

"Oh dear, not her! That wild tomboy is a memory. You'll get nothing from me now but respectful praise." Enrique looked down at his feet at the small bag he'd brought from the car. "How much time do we have?"

"There's no rush yet."

"Good, I have a present."

He reached down and brought up a slender volume in red moroccan. "I've printed only twenty of these for my dearest friends."

"What is it?"

"*The Necklace of the Dove*, the *plus ultra* erotic masterwork of Muslim Spain, translated from the colloquial Arabic of Andalusia into the Castillian tongue by your humble servant."

"How fantastic!"

"I think so. But I'm not letting the high dons at Oxford know anything about it. Its spiciness might make them change their minds about the lectureship."

"Lectureship?"

"Oriental Languages, my angel. Come this fall, my years of sweat and toil translating the classics of the East will have finally paid off."

"You must be so pleased! Eduardo, did you know about this?"

Eduardo's pouting lips turned into a scowl. "Yes, I've heard about the latest Spanish Englishman. When the eyes of the world are fixed on Spain, it follows that Enrique would escape to Oxford to instruct gangly, blond public-school boys."

"Oh, my dear! I believe you're jealous!" Enrique winked at me as he feigned mock horror at Eduardo's angry words.

Eduardo got up and pushed his chair back. "If you two will excuse me, I'm going to have a smoke."

"Remember my train leaves in forty minutes."

Eduardo nodded vaguely and shambled down the terrace toward the river.

"He's like a widow grieving over Paco," Enrique said.

"It was his first love. They were inseparable."

"Inseparable! Oh, my dear, you've been too long in Madrid! Things change even in sleepy Andalusia. Until Paco called your brother from his deathbed, they hadn't seen each other in over a year."

I must have looked surprised.

"I take it Eduardo didn't tell you. You must have thought they were still living together in Seville."

"Yes . . ."

"God, no. Paco may have left Mendoza to join Eduardo in Seville, but the little tramp ditched him within weeks. Once he was in the big city, he had little use for your brother."

"I can't believe Paco would do that. They loved each other. Eduardo thought of Paco as a . . ."

"Saint? Oh, my dear, he must have told you about that tedious game they used to play." Enrique rolled his eyes. "Your brother must really come down to earth, Angelina."

"Eduardo is a romantic with deep loyalties."

"He's an idealist, my flower, a Platonist; though he insists he's a Marxist now, 'all for the people' and all that. But there you have it. It has nothing to do with reality. The 'people' he refers to are an abstraction to be found nowhere in Spain or anywhere else. They exist solely in the mind of Eduardo Flores. The real people repel him, though he'd never admit it. He sees them as base, vulgar creatures soiling his ideal world. The very word 'proletariat' becomes hilarious in Eduardo's mouth. Can you imagine him in a factory or working the soil? He mocks me for being an aesthete, but we could stage a contest to determine which man's most devoted to exquisite taste.

"And then there's Paco. Or Saint Sebastian. A noble martyr for truth and beauty, slaughtered by the philistines, or the capitalists, or the Catholics, the Fascists, whoever's killing the saints these days. Do you know, Angelina, that Paco liked rough play?"

My head was swimming. "What do you mean?"

"He fancied tough men, my flower. Big muscular thugs, just the opposite of himself. Once he got to Seville, he couldn't get enough of them. He wore the bruises they gave him with pride."

"And Eduardo, what does he know of this?"

"Everything and nothing. He wanted to coddle and cosset Paco. Just the sort of treatment Paco couldn't stand. Once he discovered the streets, Paco would have nothing to do with his overprotective lover. Eduardo tried to hold him close. He offered him money, a place to live, undying love. All of it too dull for Saint Sebastian.

"Paco ended up as a dresser for El Zurito, Seville's washed-up *torero*. He was one of a group of slender boys who followed the bullfighters through the cafés and taverns, vying for their attention. Quite a spectacle. Eduardo and I took it in one evening at an aficionado's bar. The drunken matador and his fawning 'ladies-in-waiting,' howling and screaming, scandalizing the other patrons. Eduardo went up to Paco to say hello.

It was the first he'd seen him in months. Paco cut him dead. He pretended he didn't know your brother. Can you imagine!"

"But Paco's death. Surely, he didn't ask to be killed."

"No he didn't ask for death. Paco probably thought he could always control how far things went. The wounds would heal and the bruises would fade. But this time the game ended badly."

"Paco did ask for my brother in the end."

"In the end, yes. It almost makes me think Paco had some redeeming qualities. It gives their tragic affair a sense of resolution."

"You know, ever since I left Andalusia for the Residencia de estudiantes, I've come to think of myself as worldly. I've been exposed to so many amazing people. But all that you and Eduardo have told me makes me feel quite naive. Eduardo seems to think evil forces are undermining the forward thrust of the country. Everything is black or white with him. He sees Paco's death, even Belmonte's platitudes, as emblematic of evil."

"Well, it's tidier to think that way, my dear. Just have one portentous idea rather than a thousand messy ones. But there's some truth to what your brother says. People are choosing up sides in Spain. To what end I don't know. I do know that neither side has any use for me. It's time for your friend Enrique to adventure in more hospitable realms."

"What do you think would happen if you stayed?"

"Probably the propagandists would shred my precious copies of *The Necklace of the Dove*. If the Fascists don't hang me in Mendoza, the anarchists will get me in Barcelona. Sparing all that, my mother would bore me to death!"

"What about me? What about Eduardo?"

"I can't predict the future, my angel. I'm glad you're heading back to Madrid, and I hope you can persuade Eduardo to follow you. I'll see if I can't nudge him myself." He glanced at his pocket watch. "It's time to get you to the station. Go call your morose sibling."

WHEN WE ARRIVED AT THE STATION, Enrique greeted the stationmaster, and the two became engaged in the arcane if necessary ceremonies concerning my luggage. Eduardo and I stood together several paces away.

On the platform, two officers of the Civil Guard were questioning a couple sitting on a bench. The guardsmen's cold, rigid authority was visibly alarming to the young man and woman. The officers looked them over with fierce eyes set in expressionless faces. One of the guardsmen poked his foot at the couple's belongings, two dusty canvas sacks.

Eduardo immediately took offense. "Would you look at those bastards!" he rasped in an undertone. "Do they think those people are waiting for the train with contraband or explosives wrapped in their rags?"

"Just ignore them."

"Ignore them? How can I ignore them? They're vicious bullies."

"You're getting yourself upset. It's really not our business."

"Of course, it's our business."

"I know something of Calderón, Lope de Vega, and García Lorca. I'm an actress. I know something of modern Madrid, modern art, modern Europe. But your brand of Spanish politics, I've yet to become acquainted with."

"Well, you should be!" Eduardo looked at the guardsmen walking slowly away from the young couple. "With Paco gone, politics is more than my business. It's my duty. And don't expect irrelevant attempts at lyrical poetry from me anytime soon. From now on what I write will have to serve the people."

"Pamphleteering only addresses temporal needs, Eduardo. Poetry lasts forever. That's what Lorca says. *Duende.* Poetry touches the heart, the soul."

"Paco touched my heart and soul," Eduardo said, returning to his somber darkness.

I truly felt for my brother. "Come with me to Madrid."

"No, the fight is easy in Madrid. This is where I'm needed."

"If things are as bad in Andalusia as you suggest, I'll worry about you."

Enrique walked up and rejoined us. "All arrangements are in order, my angel. They'll treat you like royalty." He bowed and made a grand, flowing motion with his long-fingered hand.

THE CIVIL GUARDSMEN STOOD SOME DISTANCE from us in their smart green uniforms and patent-leather hats. Enrique's gesture caught their attention and they glared at us. We had grown up in Mendoza; our families were major landowners. No guardsmen had ever looked at us as they did now. They were brazen in their fixed, unblinking disapproval of our threesome. "How dare they look at us like that," I said.

Enrique stepped between Eduardo and me and put his hands on our shoulders. He smiled and spoke softly. "For them we're no longer the privileged children of wealth but two *maricóns* and an actress, upsetting the proper order of things."

"And you smile at them while they look daggers at you," said Eduardo. "It's past time for you to put away your books on Moorish Spain and think about the future!"

"My dear, I am the future! Spain's just not ready for me. Someday all the priests and grandees, the generals and shop-keepers will see the light and embrace my sensibilities. Until then, I'll bide my time on the misty isle of Albion."

Enrique looked at the guardsmen. "Admit it, Angelina. Those boys look splendid in their uniforms! How their boots and holsters shine!"

With that Enrique strode over and engaged the startled guardsmen with animated conversation about the unreliability of the train schedule and the saving beauty of the weather. The officers deferred to his astonishing confidence and his stately English tailoring. He even made them laugh.

I beamed with affection at Enrique, and Eduardo smiled for the first time since my arrival in Mendoza. He shook his head.

"Forgive my vulgarity, Angelina, but he has more balls than a regiment of the Civil Guard." He let go a laugh that was lost in the train whistle.

Eduardo grabbed my arm and fixed his eyes on mine. "I know La Barraca tours all over Spain. Tell Lorca not to come to Andalusia, not even to visit his family in Granada. I know he feels protected because his family is so established and his brother-in-law is mayor. But please, tell him not to come south! In the cafés, the taverns, even in the press, they're calling him 'the *maricón* with the bow-tie.' He'd be taking his life in his hands if he came here."

"He's famous. He's García Lorca. Who would dare touch him?"

"I'm serious, Angelina. There's great tension in Spain. Tell him not to come. Andalusia is lining up behind Franco."

I embraced my brother with his bloodshot eyes and his perfect red rose. Enrique waved his hands at the stationmaster as the train pulled in; then he turned and gave me a hug. I thanked him for his hospitality and asked him to convey my gratitude to his mother. Eduardo and Enrique assisted me in boarding the sleeping car with my carry-on. Farther down the platform the young couple boarded the third-class car under the suspicious eyes of guardsmen.

When I was comfortably seated in my cabin, I looked out the window. The train started to move. Enrique blew kisses and Eduardo signaled with a hand gesture. I waved back and felt a tug in my chest and a sudden chill. I pulled a shawl out of my bag and wrapped it tightly around me. My emotions were running from fear to joy at the thought of returning to Madrid. What would I say to Lorca? I'd been so involved in La Baracca and the newness of Madrid that I'd kept a blind eye to politics.

My visit to Mendoza had made me aware of something sinister stirring in the Spanish sand. If my brother and Enrique were right, tensions were about to erupt all over. A lot of dust was about to be kicked up and more than Paco's blood spilled.

As the station receded, the window filled with the horizon and the blue Corpus Christi sky. It was gorgeous. Nothing could duplicate the sky of Andalusia. Whatever was about to happen, it couldn't be obscured. It would remain as a blue constant, something to look up to until the dust resettled.

# Tangiers Dejoun

IT WAS GETTING ON LUNCHTIME, SO we started heading downhill towards the Grand Succo—the large plaza and marketplace at the entrance to the medina. We took a roundabout route to the Grand Succo so I could see the Teatro Cervantes one last time. It was the place in Tangiers I'd developed the most affection for. Set back from a narrow street, labeled in blue and white Spanish tile, Calle Esperanza, the theatre was a carryover from the days when Tangiers and other parts of Morocco were under Spanish rule. For the last time I looked through the wrought-iron gate at the abandoned tile and stucco building and imagined a play in progress inside—shades of Spanish actors eternally performing Lope de Vega and Calderón.

It was a short walk up from the Teatro Cervantes up Rue Salah Eddine to the Grand Succo. During the late morning to early afternoon, the Grand Succo was the only place in the city that was continuously active. I was hungry from all the walking through the *ville nouvelle* and ready to buy something for lunch to bring back to the Pension Madrid. We still had quite of few dirham to spend before we left for Spain in the morning. Richard really wanted to use some of it to score kif for our last night. One of the best places for doing that was an outside table at the Café Grand Succo, so we ordered tea and waited for someone to approach with something to sell.

When the mint tea arrived, Richard took out the ferry schedule to Algeciras and I opened my trip book to the last entry, written on the morning we'd left Rabat.

> *May 6. Bus to Tangiers. Blaring Arab radio. Heavily bandaged arm on a man in a djellaba. Man in a suit with a tambourine and flute. Nervous Spanish man, looking after two young aristocratic-looking boys, keeps getting up and down. Spectacular view of ultramarine Atlantic on the left. Field after field with row upon row of olive trees. Little white huts.*

I PUT PEN TO PAPER, BUT nothing would come. I lit another cigarette. Still nothing. It had been that way for six days. What the hell was wrong? I had so many impressions of Tangiers. Why couldn't I record them? After a few minutes, it was obvious that I wasn't going to write anything. I put the pen down and let my eyes wander over the crowd.

The Grand Succo wasn't nearly as big as the Djemaa El Fna in Marrakesh, and the makeup of the people was different. Here it was very rare to see an American or European. Other than our friend Carlton from the Yugoslavian freighter we'd taken from New York to Casablanca, and a few Europeans at the pension—we seemed to be the only visitors to the city.

I watched the comings and goings of the prosperous merchants in white djellabas and turbans, headed to midday prayers, the country women from the mountains with their striped aprons and wide-brimmed straw hats, the vendors at the stalls, and the young men in pairs, in secondhand Western clothes. I don't know why, but out on the street, I always had the impression that the people didn't want me there.

To me the people were unfriendly, often rude, and the atmosphere was so different from that of the other Moroccan cities we'd visited. Just the way the city was laid out was different. There was a more pronounced contrast between the western sector, or *ville nouvelle*, and the medina. Situated at the base of a steep, horseshoe crescent, the Europeans had claimed the highest ground—the sunny hilltops—and left the dark shadows at the base of the hills to the Moroccans. Also, in spite of the bright sunshine on the beach or the hilltops, it was always cold and windy.

I knew Morocco was devoutly Muslim, but, as I'd seen in the souks of Marrakesh, all kinds of unidentifiable things were available for the practice of *dejoun*—the local folk magic. After the Moroccan cities we'd visited, I seriously thought this inhospitable place might be under the spell of *dejoun*. When feeling most ill at ease, I thought a spell may have been cast on me. I knew it was crazy thinking, but I was reacting to something visceral. Richard blamed my unease on the kif—the strongest we'd smoked since arriving in the country almost three months ago. He was determined to get me something mild before we left.

I turned away from the crowd and looked deeply into my glass of tea, where streaks of sunlight filtered down to the bottom. It was like looking into a rusty pond where the sedge grass was mint leaves. I saw Ophelia floating in Millais's painting—her long red hair mingling with the river grasses. Her face a slowly dissolving cube of sugar. The sunlight filtered down into the glass and I began to shiver.

When a half hour passed without anyone's approaching, Richard was annoyed. "You'd think Tangiers was completely out of kif. This is the first time I've sat here without someone wanting to sell me something."

"Let's go, then. Farid is probably waiting for you on the Rue de la Plage."

"Yeah, if no one's come by now, no one's gonna come at all."

As we were gathering our things and paying the bill, Carlton, bearing a blissful smile, came out of the crowd. "Hey," I said.

"Where're you two headed?" he asked.

"We're gonna get some food and go back to the pensione."

"Good, I'll go with you."

Carlton Cartier was one of the most fascinating people I'd ever met. He was a tall, thin, elegant, light-skinned, fine-featured African American who claimed to be a full-bred Native American from a tribe in Connecticut. Richard and I had quickly struck up a friendship with him during the long hours in the bar on the freighter. Our guess was that he was his own creation—that upon boarding the ship, he'd decided to invent a new identity for himself. He didn't look at all Native American. Then again, he had a French last name, which may or may not have been authentic, and he'd once made reference to a French-Canadian heritage, possibly originating among the blacks and Native Americans of Arcadia in Nova Scotia or Newfoundland. We didn't care. His story was intriguing, and he was great company.

We'd been traveling together in Morocco since Casablanca. Today was our last day together. Unlike Richard and I who planned to travel through southern Europe, to Greece, and then back down into East Africa, Carlton was only interested in the Maghreb. After Morocco, he was going on to Tunisia and Algeria, before entering France from Oran. His ultimate goal was to get an apartment in Paris. If anyone could do it, it was Carlton. He could fit in anywhere. One of the first things he'd bought after disembarking from the freighter in Casablanca was a white-hooded djellaba. He hadn't taken it off since. He looked great in it, easily passing for a Moroccan. Lucky Carlton—on the streets he was anonymous and his French was so good, it didn't cross the local shopkeepers' minds that he was American. Only the people in the pensione knew that.

That day he'd added something new to his native look. "What's that pouch you've wearing around your neck?" I asked.

"Isn't it great? I just put it together at one of the apothecary stalls."

"So it's a magic pouch? You know that stuff freaks me out!"

"I got it for you. It's all good *dejoun*. If there's anything hostile, seen or unforeseen, a *djinn* who may be intent on causing you or Richard harm, this little packet will take care of everything!"

"Carlton, there's no such thing as good *dejoun*. It's all black magic, voodoo. People use it to hurt other people."

"I don't know where you heard that, Kate. This is all good. It's like Native American medicine—that's what I think of as magic. It's used to heal, not harm. Come, I'll show you where I got it. It's all perfectly harmless. You can put together a pouch of your own."

Despite my reluctance, Carlton led us to the apothecary stalls where sacks and sacks of herbs and oddities were stored in neat rows. Carlton began identifying everything. "This is dried lizard skin. This is dried snake. You can see they have a variety of lizard and snake skins, depending on what you need it for. This sack has pigeon talons. This is chicken talons. This sack has chips of gazelle horn. These are little felt human figures. The sacks in the back are full of herbs and pieces of bark from different trees, bird feathers. Oh, and here's the best thing— these sacks are filled with semiprecious stones."

Enthusiastically, Richard asked, "How'd you learn to identify all this?"

"I've wanted to learn ever since I saw the apothecary stalls in Marrakesh. I was intrigued by what was so reminiscent of Native American medicine. The apothecary guys in Marrakesh were always too busy to chat with me, but the guy who owns this stall has been great. He's spent hours telling me about *dejoun*. He said *dejoun* is all over the world. The ingredients vary as the flora and fauna changes."

"It's voodoo!"

"It's not voodoo, and even voodoo gets a bad rap. You've got to look beyond the chicken blood. Yes, some people use magic or medicine to bring harm to others, but most people use it to bring about something good—good health, wealth, love, a pregnancy, or protection from those who might want to cause harm. *Dejoun* is a way to empower yourself—to bring about a desired effect, to sway someone, to keep a bad *djinn* at bay."

"This guy's pulling your leg. He's got you totally convinced that most people use it for good things."

"It's true, Kate. It's white magic. The people who use it to cause harm are a minority. If they're trying to cause harm, it has to be a personal thing, a vendetta. You have nothing to worry about. You don't know anyone in Tangiers."

"I know some people."

"Who, Señora Garcia at the pensione?"

"I don't think she likes it when I go out alone with you—her pet 'chocolate.'"

"She's just teasing," Carlton said.

"There's Farid. I don't trust him."

"Babe, Farid adopted us at the bus station. He found us the pensione in the medina. Plus he's been a good drug connection."

"Oh, forget Farid," Carlton said. "He watches too many gangster movies. Here, let's make a protective pouch for you. You'll feel better the instant you put it on."

"I don't want a pouch. You said the pouch you're wearing is for my protection. If there's any truth in any of this, I should be safe with that."

"I'll make a second pouch. Then you'll be doubly protected."

I watched as Carlton lead Richard and I from sack to sack, filling a pouch with a small felt figure, yellow snakeskin, palm bark, a falcon feather, a small turquoise stone, a small piece of amethyst, and several different herbs or dried leaves. When the pouch was full, he paid the vendor.

"All I need now is something from you for the pouch—a piece of clothing, something you wear every day, like a piece of jewelry, or it can be a strand of hair."

"I'm not cooperating with this madness."

"Katie, your whole sense of Tangiers as a place possessed is madness. We can change all that."

"Ouch, that hurt, you shit." While my back was turned, Carlton had yanked a strand of my hair from the root. "I'll kill you! Please, before I pass out, can we get some food!"

We went to the food stalls and picked up bread, goat's cheese, tomatoes, and bottled water.

As expected, when we got back to the pensione, Farid was waiting in the narrow shadows of the Rue de la Page. Despite his emulation of Americans and Europeans, as indicated by his denim jeans, jacket, and long hair, I felt he despised us. Richard got along well with him, as did Carlton, but he gave me a bad vibe.

"Babe, could I have the packages? I'm going inside."

"Knock on my door when you're ready to go to dinner," Carlton said.

Upstairs in our pale blue room I took my copy of *The Big Sleep* out of its bag. I'd purchased it that morning at the Librairie des Colonnes, the best French-English bookstore in the city. I felt better just looking at it. The cover was brilliant. The greater portion of the artwork was a color-tinted still of Bogart and Bacall from the film adaptation. All the lettering was lime green, as was the shirt under Bogie's black suit. Bacall had per-fectly parted lemon-yellow hair, a suit with lime-green trim, blue eyes, and lustrous red lips. The quote on the back cover was perfect: Philip Marlowe was neat, clean, shaved and sober, and he didn't care who knew it. . . My first impulse had been to buy two copies—one to read and one to keep as an object of adoration. Unfortunately, I only had one carrying case to get me from Tangiers, to the Serengeti and back to New York.

An acknowledgment on the back cover read, "The covers of this series incorporate material supplied by courtesy of Twentieth Century-Fox, Warner Bros. and RKO Pictures. Inside the back cover was a list of all the titles in the series, including the other Chandlers. As I was imagining an armed George Raft in a lemon-yellow trench coat for the cover of *Farewell My Lovely*, Richard came into the room.

"You look happy."

"I have something that's going to make you happy."

"Mild kif?"

"So mild, Farid gave it to me. He says it's not worth smoking."

"Oh, then it must be good."

Richard handed me a little yellow parchment packet filled with pale green leaves ground to a powder. "Marrakesh kif!"

I threw my arms around his neck and pulled him down to kiss him. He sat down next to me and put his arm around me. "He's got 'double-o' from Ketama, too. It's supposed to be the best high in Morocco! I have to meet him later at the Café Fuentes to pick it up."

"Oh, babe, I know you've been dying to try it . . ."

"All this time in Morocco the legendary 'double-o' has eluded me. Now on my last night in Tangiers, I'm finally going to have some!"

"Babe, I'm happy for you. I really am. I just worry that Farid will mess things up as so often happens with him. He'll turn this into a long drawn-out affair, and we'll wind up spending hours in the Petit Succo. I wanted to spend a quiet last night with Carlton. Maybe have dinner at the Hotel Minza. Can't Farid bring it here?"

"No, he insists we meet him in the souk. Carlton's coming, too. He wants to buy some."

I didn't like the idea, but I didn't want to impinge on Richard's obvious excitement. The Petit Succo, a small part of the souk in the heart of the medina, freaked me out more than any other place in the city. It had come as such a disappointment. It was the place I most wanted to see in Tangiers. Some of our favorite writers had been there, lived there. While I didn't expect to see Bowles, Genet, Burroughs, or Ginsberg wandering around, I hoped we'd catch a glimpse of what had initially attracted them to the place. We went almost daily, and after six days, I was still searching for that elusive something. Most of the cafés the Beats frequented were now gone, as were the brothels and drug dens. Without the air of permissiveness that existed when Tangiers was an international city, all that remained was a deserted, shadow-filled labyrinth. Compared with the sunlit explosion of color in Marrakesh—the abundance of rugs, scarves, clothes, jewelry and people—the Petit Succo looked like it was going out of business.

I laid the food out on a sheet of newspaper on the nightstand between our twin beds. I sliced the tomato and cheese, broke the flat bread in half, and opened our big bottle of water.

Richard dipped the bowl of his *sebsi* into the parchment packet and filled it with kif. He lit the pipe and drew deeply on the long, wooden stem before closing his eyes and resting his head on the wall behind his bed. A few moments passed and he drew again, then he extended the pipe to me. "I think you're going to like this." I was hesitant to inhale, and Richard sensed it. "Really, babe, it's your kind of kif." I trusted Richard more than I trusted anyone, but I didn't trust Farid—so my first hit was a short one. I wanted to test my reaction. All the kif I'd had so far in Tangiers created heat and pressure in my temples that spread throughout my head—a dull heat and pressure that lingered in my skull, never lightening my spirits or extending a trace of warmth to the rest of my body.

"Well?" Richard asked.

"So far, so good."

"Oh, I'm so glad." Richard leaned over and gave me a kiss. "I didn't want you to leave here feeling badly. Have some more."

"No, no, let me wait. I don't want to push it. This is nice."

We ate our fresh lunch. Richard had more kif, then came over to my bed. Enhanced by the warm feeling created by the kif, we made love. Being entwined with Richard took me out of my head and let me focus on my body. What a relief to leave all those swirling, negative thoughts behind, replaced by touching, licking, and kissing. I felt tingly and relaxed at the same time. When we'd climaxed on one of the twin beds, Richard drowsily asked me to try on my bathing suit.

"If I do that, you're gonna want to make love again."

"Oh, the horror . . ."

We both laughed as I got up and pulled my red bikini out of its bag—another purchase that morning. We'd both bought swimsuits because we planned to spend a few weeks in St. Tropez. Richard bought brown, European-style swimming briefs, which I knew he'd look great in. I'd bought the only thing that was available in my size—a bright red bikini. Red wasn't my color. I didn't think it was flattering because I was a fair-skinned redhead. I put it on and looked at myself in the mirror over the dresser. Aside from my face and arms, I was pale white. When I turned around to show Richard, he was sound asleep. He looked so content, I didn't disturb him. I'd always envied his ability to nap wherever he was—something I rarely, if ever, did. Rather than getting back into bed with him, I pulled my blue djellaba from Marrakesh out of a drawer. As I did so, a small object came flying out of the drawer with the djellaba. I reached down to the floor to pick it up. It was a felt human figure with a red cord around its neck and broken toothpicks jammed into its skull. I totally freaked. It looked so sinister and confirmed all my fears about *dejoun*. I hadn't opened that drawer in a few days, but it wasn't there then. I'd never seen it before! How'd it get there? Who put it there? The paranoia that had subsided came rushing back. My thoughts were rushing. My heart beating.

"Richard!" I half cried, half screamed.

Slowly he opened his eyes and turned toward me. He was groggy and didn't pick up on my distress. All he noticed was the bikini. "Katie, come here. You look beautiful . . ."

"Richard!"

This time he sensed my panic. "Babe, what's the matter? What's wrong?"

I showed him the figurine.

"Where'd you get that?"

"It was in my drawer when I took out my djellaba. I opened that draw the other day. It's never been there before!"

"Okay, okay . . . bring it here. Come sit down. Let me see it."

I was in tears. "Babe, babe, it's nothing. It's a little doll. I bet Carlton put it there. He probably slipped it in for extra protection."

"Extra protection?! It's got a rope around its neck and spikes in its head! It's me! I know it's me! It's a replica of me!"

Richard put his arms around me and held me tight. "We'll ask Carlton about it when we see him. He'll be able to explain it. Who knows? Maybe it was in that drawer when we first moved in and you just didn't see it. Maybe some tourist left it behind."

"No, it was put there for me. I know it. It's what I've been saying about Tangiers. All this unease is for a reason. It's the *dejoun* thing. Someone wants to harm me. I want to leave. I want to leave right now."

"Babe, we can't leave. The ferries don't start running again until the morning. Just let me get the 'double-o.' After that we can have dinner at the Minza and spend the night there." By now I was shaking. "Here, let's put your djellaba on and get you under the covers next to me."

I let Richard's body and soothing words wash over me. It was his calm at that moment that kept me from giving in entirely to fear. He dipped the sebsi again into the yellow packet, lit the bowl, and took a long hit. He handed the lit pipe to me. I was so physically and emotionally limp, I let him direct me. I took the pipe and inhaled longer than I had before. With Richard's arms around me and the warm smoke inside me, I started to relax. With the hysteria gone from my voice I started to tell him about a dream I'd had during the Atlantic crossing. I dreamed of a pink horse. The horse was actually a white stallion standing in the desert at sunrise. Its pink color was a reflection of the red desert mountains around it. On the ship when I'd woken from the dream, I felt brave, clean, optimistic. I took it to be a good omen. With that image focused behind my closed eyes, I floated out of Richard's arms, mounted the stallion, and rode into a shallow sleep.

RICHARD WOKE ME WITH A SOFT kiss. He'd just returned from the shower down the hall. "You slept for a while, babe. You needed that."

"What time is it?"

"Close to six. We have to meet Farid at seven."

"I should take a shower."

I grabbed a towel, soap, shampoo and headed down the hall. The water hitting my skin felt like pellets of ice. It shook me out of my slumbers and the image of the *dejoun* doll came flashing back. In the room I immediately brought it up to Richard. "It's gonna be okay. I'd never let anything happen to you. We'll show it to Carlton. I'm sure he'll have a reasonable explanation."

My imagination now racing again, I dressed quickly, pulling on my uniform—khaki slacks, black turtleneck, and soft red shoes from Marrakesh.

Richard was wearing his usual uniform—jeans, a black tee shirt, Frye boots, and a combat jacket. Richard had acquired a deep, golden tan during our stay in Morocco. Coupled with his dark brown shoulder-length hair, he'd never looked more beautiful.

When we were ready, we knocked on Carlton's door. There he was, covered head to toe in his white djellaba, wearing yellow shoes similar to my red ones, and the two *dejoun* pouches.

Richard pulled out the little figure.

"Oh, how neat! Where'd you get that?"

Richard told him the story. Carlton didn't offer much by way of an explanation other what Richard had suggested. "It's probably been there all along. You know how things get shifted around."

"No, Carlton," I said. "This is bad *dejoun*. I can feel it."

"Well, I don't agree with you, but if you don't want it, I'll take it."

I took it out of Richard's hand and gave it to Carlton. "Take it, it's yours."

At the front reception desk Señora Garcia asked where we were going. "Café Fuentes," Carlton said.

"Oh, very good, very good café for chocolate."

By the time we reached the street, the sun was setting and the cold, sharp blades of wind had yet to be sheathed in the oncoming night. We walked down to the beach and turned left onto the narrow extension of street that ran below the old walls of the medina. There wasn't a soul in sight. The only sound was the sound of our footsteps as we mounted the stone steps that lead to the ramparts at the top of the old walls. From there we took the Rue des Postes to the Petit Succo.

Farid was waiting outside the café with a friend wearing purple sunglasses. He pulled Richard and Carlton aside and spoke with them in a huddle. "Richard came back to me and said, "Farid doesn't want you to come with us."

"You mean he doesn't have the stuff with him? This is ridiculous. I can't stay here by myself. Why do you have to go somewhere else?"

"His friend with the shades has the 'double-o,' and he doesn't want a Western woman coming to his house."

"Oh God, this is so typical of Farid. He has to complicate everything. Do you have to have the 'double-o'? Really, I don't want to stay here by myself."

"Farid was good enough to give me the mild stuff for nothing. I can't turn down his offer."

Carlton came over. "Is everything okay?"

"Kate's afraid to stay here by herself."

"We're not going to be long. Farid's friend lives right off the Petit Succo. I'll leave this with you," Carlton said, removing one of the pouches from around his neck.

"Carlton, after what's just happened, do you really think I want to wear that?"

"Here," he said, putting it into my satchel. "Just hold on to it. You'll be fine in the Café Fuentes."

"Oh Christ."

Richard put his arm around me and kissed me. "Babe, we're gonna be a few minutes."

I watched Richard and Carlton walk across the square and follow Farid and his friend through a narrow passageway. When they were out of sight, I went into the café. I went upstairs and took a table by the front windows so I could look down on the square. I felt quite vulnerable, alone at night in the souk, where women—Moroccan or Western—were never seen alone. Even with a male companion, one wasn't entirely protected. A week before, in Rabat, a small boy had walked up to me and grabbed my crotch while I walked with Richard. Plus before leaving on the freighter I'd heard a story about a friend of a friend, a single woman, being raped in Agadir.

From a radio mounted on the opposite wall, the shrill, guttural sound of Arab pop music flooded the room.

"Señorita!"

I jumped at the sudden sound from the Spanish waiter looming behind me. He had an order pad and pencil propped on his belly. I wanted a drink, but alcohol was forbidden in the medina, so I ordered an orange soda. I also asked him if he could bring me a pencil and a piece of paper. I hadn't brought a book or notebook because I didn't think I'd need anything. The waiter bowed and smiled lasciviously, then walked back to the counter.

Alone for the first time in the Fuentes, I had the chance to really look at the place. The walls were a pale shade of green, lacquered with decades of cigarette smoke. They were decorated with a portrait of King Hassan, photographs of Arab recording artists, and Pepsi ads. Fluorescent lighting illuminated an array of Formica tabletops with the ubiquitous red, white, and blue Cinzano ashtrays I'd seen throughout Morocco. The old ceiling fan was motionless, its function taken over by a single standing electric fan. Like the ceiling fan, the clock on the wall was also dead—its arms stuck forever at three twenty-five. By myself, at night, everything looked shabby. I'd liked it the first time we went there for lunch, thinking it held a bit of the hip debauchery I was looking for. Now I was at a loss to find anything likable about the place.

The waiter brought the soda, paper, and pencil. He bowed, smiled lasciviously, and walked back to the counter.

While I sipped my soda and drew pyramids on the paper, a stray dog entered the café, walked upstairs and came directly over to me. The poor thing was emaciated, but his tail was wagging. He was so sweet and friendly. In spite of his mangy condition, I patted him on the head. He sat at my feet and looked up at me with soulful eyes. A new companion. That's how I thought of him. Someone to stay by my side until Richard came back. He was far more protection than the damned pouch in my satchel. I decided to call him Sebsi.

"Sebsi, you hungry?" He looked at me with that adorable crooked head dogs have when they don't quite understand what you're saying.

I reached in my satchel to see if I had money to buy Sebsi a sandwich. A bolt of adrenaline shot through me when I realized I didn't have a cent. That night Richard was carrying all the money. Knowing I was not only alone but penniless made me feel more vulnerable than ever. My alarm brought blood pulsing back to my temples. Suddenly, my head was a globe of hot gas. Should something go wrong, I had no money to curry help. I was stuck there waiting, and already more than a few minutes had passed.

I looked toward the counter. The waiter was standing, chatting in Spanish with a rough-looking local. He leered at me with a gap-toothed smile.

This is unbearable, I thought.

More time passed.

The top floor began to fill up. The waiter brought mint tea to an old man in a threadbare suit at one table and mint tea to two older British men whom I'd never seen before. They sat at the table next to mine and attempted to strike up a conversation. I was so nervous, I was convinced they were trying to pick me up. I was also afraid they'd alert the waiter to Sebsi's presence.

I looked over at the counter. The gap-toothed man was now chatting with Farid's friend with the purple sunglasses. I looked out the window to see if Richard, Farid, and Carlton were entering the café. They weren't. I didn't know what to think. Richard was to have scored his 'double-o' at the guy with the purple sunglasses' house a while ago. Behind his shades, I felt the man's eyes look right through me. The man with the gap teeth spoke to Purple Shades in Arabic and laughed. Purple Shades was expressionless. He continued to stare at me. The waiter came over and spoke to the two men in Spanish. The waiter and the gap-toothed man laughed and I heard one of them say "*puta*."

At that my palms became wet. The radio was blaring. The lighting was so intense. The waiter and the gap-toothed man watched from the counter as Purple Shades started walking toward me. I reached down and felt for Sebsi. He was still there.

I stood up before the man reached me and threw Carlton's pouch on the table. I stood up so abruptly, my leg slammed the edge of the table, almost knocking it over. It disturbed Sebsi, who got to his feet. I knocked the chair over as I headed towards the stairs, followed by my companion. I was breathing so heavily, I thought I might expel all my breath. I couldn't speak. I couldn't call for help. Just like in a dream, that mechanism was paralyzed. Somehow—and I'm sure it was because of Sebsi—I reached the bottom of the staircase and pushed and shoved my way out the front door of the Fuentes, followed by the waiter.

Outside I stopped still and bent over like a long-distance runner to catch my breath. Looking down I saw a pair of Frye boots. "Richard!" I stood up and pressed my face against his chest.

"Katie, what's going on? You look like a ghost!"

"Did something happen?" Carlton asked.

Behind me the waiter was haranguing in Spanish. "Richard, please pay him," I said. "I had an orange soda. And pay him for a bowl of water and a sandwich for Sebsi."

"Sebsi?"

"Sebsi, my little adopted pooch. That's who protected me, Carlton, not your damned pouch."

"You can't believe that."

"I certainly do. I left the damned pouch upstairs."

"I'm going to get it."

"Don't you dare. I don't want to have anything more to do with this magic shit!"

"Richard, tell the waiter we're not leaving until he brings water and food for Sebsi."

Richard spoke with the waiter and handed him what must have been a nice wad of dirham. He left with a smile and returned shortly with a bowl of water and kebabs for Sebsi.

Richard started explaining the delay. "Farid took us on this wild goose chase . . ."

"Please, babe, can it wait till we're out of here? I have to get out of here."

I gave Sebsi a farewell pat on the head. He was busily gobbling up the first good meal he'd had in weeks. Soon we were on the ramparts heading back to the pensione.

"So, like I was saying . . . Farid dragged us all over the medina. First he took us to the guy with the purple sunglasses' house. He didn't have anything, but he said someone was coming with the 'double-o.'"

"We waited there forever," Carlton said. "Then Farid took us to two other houses, but they turned up empty as well. When he said the next stop was the Kasbah, we both put our feet down. We'd never been out that far. It was starting to get a little too weird, and if Farid dumped us out there, we wouldn't know our way back to the Fuentes."

I stopped while we were still on the ramparts. My heart had stopped palpitating and my breathing returned to normal. "All I have to say is no more medina tonight. I want to go back to the pensione, get our stuff, pay up, and leave, then head straight for the Minza. I want a nice final meal with Carlton. I want to share a bottle of wine. I want a hot shower, warm bed, and I want to leave on the first ferry in the morning!"

"Sure babe, we can do that. I've got American Express checks for the Minza."

"Great Carlton, there's just one thing I ask of you. Just for tonight, just while you're still in my company, please get rid of whatever *dejoun*, magic, medicine crap you still have. As soon as we leave you can get all new stuff, but tonight, while you're with me, for my sanity's sake . . ."

I breathed a long, deep sigh as my friend threw his remaining pouch and the felt figure over the ramparts.

# Novalis

*The Night is here –*
*My soul's enraptured –*
*The earthly day's past*
*And you're mine again.*

— *Georg Friedrich von Hardenberg*

IT WAS A RAINY DAY IN late September. The wind was nasty, getting down around the neck, up the sleeves, and under the waist of my new leather jacket. In the open space of Times Square, the light offered little contrast to the dimness of the subway stairwell from which I'd emerged. It was my birthday, and I'd elected to cut classes at Roslyn High School and spend the money my father mailed me at Lou Tannen's Magic Shop.

I flipped up my collar and walked up Broadway, catching a glimpse of John Wayne blowing smoke rings out of the big cigarette billboard. In the gray drizzle, a few guys my age huddled together looking at Cuban boots in Florsheim's window. At the Howard Johnson's a group of suburban housewives jostled their way through the door, no doubt intent on having a grilled cheese or BLT before seeing Burton and Taylor in *Cleopatra*.

*The Birds* was playing at the movie house next door to Lou Tannen's. In the display stills outside the theater, Tippi Hedren and Rod Taylor locked eyes over a caged bird, hundreds of sparrows flew through a fireplace, and crows swooped and attacked a group of school children. Definitely, *The Birds* was the film I most wanted to see of the new releases. But that would be another day.

The warm air in the vestibule at 1540 Broadway was a nice change from the wet street. I took the stairs to the second floor and opened the door with the panel of frosted glass stenciled with a gold top hat and cane. Inside there was one customer for whom the one salesman, Jack Miller, was demonstrating the Zombie Ball. I'd run into Jack over the Labor Day weekend on the boardwalk in Coney Island. We were both there to catch Novalis's act. During an intermission, he came up to me and told me I might want to stop by the shop and see the new items that had come in.

Jack gave a wink to indicate that he'd be with me momentarily. I signaled not to hurry. Ordinarily, when I visited Tannen's it was on a Saturday afternoon and the place was mobbed. I'd never seen it on a Monday morning, quiet and near empty, and for the first time I was getting a good look at the mural and the posters on the walls. Houdini in chains. Blackstone and Thurston in formal evening dress and black capes. Chung Ling Soo defying bullets. Framed handbills for *The Hour of Darkness* at the Egyptian Hall Bazaar, the *Wonders of the Enchanted Palace,* and *Davenport's Spirit Cabinet.* The mural was total kitsch but wonderful. In lurid red, yellow, orange and pink paint mellowed with age, it depicted a winged genie hovering over a snake charmer and a silver urn emanating wisps of smoke. It was the perfect backdrop for a place that was part funhouse, part treasure trove.

The customer was having difficulty grasping the mechanics of the Zombie Ball. He repeatedly asked Jack to perform the trick, and each time Jack cheerfully obliged. He showed both sides of the foulard outstretched between his hands over a polished metal ball resting on a stand. He covered the ball with the foulard for a second. Then the ball rose through the air and disappeared behind his shoulder. It was one of my favorite tricks to perform at kids' parties, though I doubted my performances had Jack's panache.

While the demonstration continued, I checked out the display case labeled CLUB AND STAGE MAGIC—NEW ARRIVALS. Side by side, with printed cards describing their effects, were such items as Great Brahman Rice Bowls, Rosini's Robot Wand, Flames of Aladdin, and Snows of Kimalatong. For their names alone, I wanted to buy each one and keep them in mint condition in their original boxes in my bedroom where I could marvel at them whenever I wanted.

The guy for whom Jack was demonstrating finally got it. He left the shop, having laid out $19.50 for a deluxe model, seven-inch Zombie and an additional $2.50 for a red foulard to go with it. With a satisfied look on his face, Jack closed the cash register and came over to where I was standing.

"See anything you like, Joe?"

"Well," I said, "I like everything, but I can't afford it all." He asked me how much I wanted to spend. My father had sent me a twenty, but I didn't want to blow it all at Tannen's.

"Fifteen," I said.

"Fifteen. No problem." He slid open the back of the display case. "Great Brahman Rice Bowls, Sands of the Desert, and The Famous Egg Bag are all less than fifteen. Nesto Candles—for one hand only—is ten."

"How much is the Wrist Guillotine?"

"Seventeen-fifty."

"And the Fire Bowl?"

"Twenty-one."

"Okay," I said, "let me see the Rice Bowls and Flames of Aladdin."

Jesus! Decisions. Both items were twelve-fifty, and whereas the Great Brahman Rice Bowls was a new version of a venerable stage trick, the gaudy brass Aladdin's lamp was irresistible. I read the trick's description on the ornate printed card: "Really sensational! A dream come true! As though a real GENI were present, the flames leave the lamp and FLOAT in mid-air!!!" I *had* to have it. With the money left over, I bought a new Lucite wand to replace the one some brat had walked off with at a Glen Cove birthday party.

Jack Miller took my money and put the wand and the Flames of Aladdin in a shiny black bag with Tannen's cool, gold-printed logo. He handed me my change, and taking me by surprise, asked if I wanted to join him for lunch. It threw me off a little. I mean, I hardly knew the guy. Some of the other dudes who frequented the shop told me Jack was gay. I came from a white-bread Long Island town where anyone who was queer never copped to it. So what would I say if he came on to me? I gave it a minute and thought, What the fuck? It didn't matter. Jack was a good guy who was full of the fun and mystery of magic tricks. Fact is, I didn't think there was anything wrong with being gay. The only people who said so always turned out to be assholes. Fuck 'em.

Jack called me out of my meditation. "Hey Joe! Lunch?"

"Sure, Jack, lunch would be cool."

"Great! You pick the place."

Other than Howard Johnson's, I was only familiar with one other place in the neighborhood—the place where my father and I ate before going to boxing matches or hockey games at the Garden. "How about the Alamo Chili Café?"

"The Alamo it is! Just let me close up and we're off to eat Mexican."

Down on the street, there were a few more people hastening in the rain on their lunch breaks. Jack Miller opened a big green umbrella and welcomed me to share it with him. Jack was almost a foot shorter than I was. I bent to get under, then we were off.

"Yah know, Joe," Jack said, half trotting to keep up with my pace, "We can make this a leisurely lunch. On a Monday afternoon with weather like this, the shop's dead. Lou's down in Miami. So we can relax and shoot the breeze."

At Forty-seventh Street we crossed Broadway, heading east. The Alamo Chili Café was between Sixth and Seventh, in the middle of the block. It had been a while since I'd been there, but *nothing* had changed. The framed page from the *New York Mirror* was there near the entrance, with Dan Parker's article about Casey Stengel, eating at the Alamo. The long, black wood bar was still on the left, and the red malt shop–style booths on the right. It was a simple place with a funky, B-movie Mexican look.

Only one or two people sat at the bar and all the booths were empty. I led the way to the one in the rear beneath a yellow velvet sombrero with filigree trimming. We slid into opposite seats, and a guy came over to take our orders. He spoke slowly and had a sleepy Tijuana look in his eyes. I ordered my favorite—spaghetti with chili and two tamales. Jack ordered the same and asked if he could have a drink while we waited for our meal.

"Si, señor," said the Mexican, with a definite Rio Grande accent. "What will it be?"

"Scotch on the rocks."

"Scotch on the rocks, *si*." He turned his glance to me. "And you, señor?"

"I'll have a Coke."

The waiter walked away and both Jack and I were silent, settling in after our rain rush. The beverages arrived quickly; once

Jack had a sip or two of his scotch, he started talking in his Noo Yawk voice. I was all ears for what he had to say.

"So, you're a Novalis fan. Probably, I should put that in the past tense. You know he's gone missing. Since Labor Day, no one's seen him."

"No kiddin'?" I said. "Man, that's weird."

Jack shifted into a more serious tone. "It is. He really has disappeared into thin air. Gone without a trace. And this morning two police detectives came into the shop to quiz me. Thank god Lou's in Miami! I didn't know what he would want me to tell them. I doubt that I know much more about what happened than the cops. From talking to the detectives, I got the bad impression that they're working on a murder case. I had my suspicions, too. But I wasn't thinking it was that bad." His words stung me, shocked me. I'd only discovered Novalis at the beginning of the summer. A friend of mine had taken me to see him perform in a dive on Surf Avenue. He was amazing. A master illusionist with a cool, almost indifferent stage manner and leading-man looks. He looked like a young Robert Mitchum, only more slightly built. I wondered what the hell he was doing in a dive in Coney Island. He was so fucking good. Good enough for *The Ed Sullivan Show*. Good enough for Broadway with tickets sold out six months in advance. Later in the summer he moved into the Squire Room, a slightly less-seedy club. It was a step up, but still. . .

"Who would want to kill Novalis?" I felt very strange asking Jack that question.

"Christ, I don't know. He was involved in all kinds of freaky entanglements. We were supposed to get together that night, after his last show of the summer. I waited for him in his dingy room in the Sea Beach Hotel. The last show was scheduled to end at eleven thirty. I smoked half a pack of Luckies waiting for him. When he still hadn't shown at one o'clock, I took the subway back to Manhattan.

"In the morning, Anita, the daughter of the guy who runs the Squire, called me at home to ask if Novalis was with me. Much to Daddy's distaste, Anita had become Novalis's stage assistant and lover during the Squire Room engagement. She was crazy about him.

"Anita said there'd been a bizarre twist in the Substitution Trunk trick at the end of the last show. You've seen the act. The assistant gets in a box, which is chained up and secured with a real steel lock. The box is lowered into a huge travel trunk, which is also chained and locked. Novalis raises a curtain around himself and the trunk. With a count of *one, two, three,* the curtain drops, and, voilà, there stands the assistant, free and out of the trunk. The magician is gone. The trunk is still locked and tied. The assistant opens the trunk and then the box. Out steps Novalis, having switched places with the assistant in an instant. Right? That's the trick. A real pisser. But when Anita opened the box there was no one inside to step out!"

"Thanks," I said, as the waiter placed a large plate of spaghetti with chili and tamales in front of me. Jack looked at his serving with something less than relish and ordered another scotch.

"Anita was completely freaked. Novalis had never said anything about vanishing. She had to think fast and improvise her way off the stage. No one knows how he could possibly have exited the trunk because his methods were all his own. No one else was in on the secret—sure as hell not me. Afterward, no one saw him back stage or in the dressing room. Anita and the guys who work for her old man made a frantic round of Novalis's regular Coney haunts. He wasn't with Fat Tina. He wasn't with Phil, who operates the Cyclone. He wasn't at the tattoo parlor or any of the bars. By the time they got to the Sea Beach, I was long gone. Back home asleep."

Jack Miller's second drink arrived and he took a lusty gulp. "It was bizarre. But then again, it wasn't a complete surprise. I'd come to anticipate the unexpected with Novalis. My first thought was that his disappearance was his idea of a joke, the mysterious grand finale of the season. But after a week passed and *still* no one had seen or heard from him, I began to get anxious. I began to think about him committing suicide."

I must have looked stunned because Jack repeated himself.

"That's right, Joe. I began to think suicide, because it made sense. Knowing Novalis as well as I did, it made sense. You see, he confided in me. He told me things he would never tell anyone else. I knew he wanted out of his relationship with Anita and out of his business association with her mobbed-up family. He felt obliged to them because of the cash they'd put into his act. Big money for top-drawer stuff like the Substitution Trunk and the White Cargo Cage. For once, he had a first class act and he was starting to attract serious attention. You could smell success and big recognition coming his way. But, yah know, I think the idea of sudden fame scared him, that and the fact that he would owe it to Anita and her father.

"No, fame and wealth didn't fit into Novalis's overall picture of things. It would have been too much of an infringement on his freedom. It would have cramped his style. You gotta understand, Joe, he was a drifter at heart, and I think he wanted to keep it that way. Drifting from place to place, with nothing but an old obsession to keep him company."

I was amazed that Jack was telling me all this. Like I said, I hardly knew the guy, and we were getting into pretty deep waters.

"Do you know what Novalis's real name is? Homer Sinclair Nash. Can you believe it? It's a southern thing. I think his family had money. He's from somewhere in Georgia. He took the name Novalis after a poet he was hung up on. Once he told me that he thought he might be the reincarnation of this poet. The real Novalis was an eighteenth-century German. He died at the age of twenty-nine, just a few years after the death of the woman he loved. Do you know how old our Novalis is? Twenty-nine! And he'd been engaged to a girl who died tragically a few years ago."

I leaned forward, an enthralled kid listening to Jack Miller talk about life and death.

"It happened down South. Homer was just starting out. He wasn't Novalis then; he was just Homer, Master of Mystery. He'd hooked up with a carnival in a little town near Savannah. One night a beautiful girl from the local high school came to his show with some of her girlfriends. Her name was Donna. She was the daughter of the local sheriff. Homer was usually indifferent to his admirers, but he *noticed* this girl. From the stage, he looked over at her throughout his act. Each time their eyes met. After the show, Donna separated herself from her friends and waited for him. As Novalis describes it, it was a once-in-a-lifetime experience. He told me that standing before her, looking into her eyes, was like being in the presence of the other half of his soul.

"Shortly after their first meeting, Donna and Homer became lovers. It was the first time for Donna, and it wasn't easy for her. She had to steal away from her friends and family and lie about where she was going. She was terrified that her father would find out about Homer and their secret trysts. By the end of the summer she was pregnant. Novalis wanted to marry her. They planned to elope when the carnival packed it up. Then something awful happened.

"For all his love of his soul mate, Novalis couldn't control his sexual appetites. Women and men were drawn to him like moths to a flame, and he couldn't reject their attention. One night Donna came earlier than usual for a rendezvous. She went behind Novalis's tent and found him getting a hand job from one of the carnie midgets. She let out a scream and ran out into the crowd on the fairgrounds. Novalis took off after her. When he caught up with her, she was standing in a seat stopped at the top of the Ferris wheel. He pleaded with her to calm down, to sit down, to come down and talk to him. He shouted that everything was all right, nothing had changed.

She must have been devastated, in a state of shock, because she began to rock the seat, violently, back and forth. Whether by accident or intent she tumbled out and fell to her death. After that night, Homer Sinclair Nash fled the town and the carnival and started a new life as Novalis. He had the names Novalis and Donna tattooed in a black heart on his chest. Then he started drifting up the coast."

Jack waved to the waiter and raised his glass. He hadn't touched his spaghetti, chili, or tamales. I'd finished my plate and was still hungry. I ordered the one item on the menu offered as dessert—guava jelly and cream cheese on saltine crackers.

Jack went on with a faraway look on his face. "I first met Novalis about a year ago when he started coming into the shop. He wanted books on the great illusionists and the history of stage magic. Right away, I sensed something special about him. We became friendly. We started having lunch together. Novalis needed a confidant. I don't think he'd ever had someone to speak to about what had happened. For whatever reason, he decided that I was the one to listen to his story.

"I remember one night in particular. He was still working Surf Avenue. We took a walk on the boardwalk. He was going on and on about infinity and the place where the night sky and the ocean come together. He said he wanted to go there and be reunited with Donna. He was writing a lot of poetry. We stopped beneath a lamplight and he took a poem out of his pocket to read to me. You know, Joe, a guy like me doesn't know much about poetry, but I thought it sounded pretty good. Different. Distinctive. It was all about love, sacrifice, the night. He was very much into 'the night.' In retrospect, I think the poetry I heard that night foretold everything that's come down."

Jack Miller reached into his pocket and took out something handwritten on a sheet of yellow legal paper.

"I think this is Novalis's suicide note. It was in his room the night he disappeared. I think he asked me to meet him there, fully knowing he'd never come, but knowing I'd find this poem. If you don't mind, I'd like you to read it."

I felt privileged and nervous at the same time. Goose bumps rippled all over me. I put down my cracker and picked up the paper. In small, blue block letters, printed with a ballpoint pen, I read.

### HYMN TO THE NIGHT

*Down at last to the sea*
*At last to drown my soul*
*The distant lights of the carnival*

*The noise of the crowd*
*The notes of the calliope*
*Rise high above the waves*

*On a pedestal shell*
*My Venus comes*
*With open arms*
*To sleep with her, her long sleep*

*Now, loving eyes and forgiveness*
*As I shed my shirt—*
*the veined wings of a mourning dove—*
*And offer myself to the Night*

It wasn't Corso but it sounded okay to me. It sounded pretty sad, like it might have been a farewell. "Yeah, I see what you mean," I said. "I can see why you would think these were his last words."

Jack Miller was visibly pleased, maybe moved by my reaction. "You know," he said, "once I'd come to that conclusion, about a week after the disappearance I went out to Coney Island. The weather was like it is today, the beach was deserted. I had to walk way out past the last pier before I found what I was looking for—Novalis's translucent, dark blue shirt, embroidered with white stars. It was washed up under the boardwalk."

"You're fuckin' kiddin' me! Did you tell the cops? Do they know about the poem? Or Anita? Does she know anything about the shirt or the poem?"

"No. Exposing the secret of Homer Sinclair Nash's final deception doesn't seem right to me. I don't know if you get this, but to expose it would be unpardonable. Everything I've told you belongs to Novalis and Donna, wherever they are."

I saw his point. "But haven't you just exposed the secret to me?"

"You're different, Joe. I can trust you."

Our lunch had now taken up the better part of two hours and I was feeling edgy because I had a train to catch back to Long Island. Jack finished his drink and signaled the waiter to bring the check. "This is on me, Joe," he said. He thanked me for listening and urged me to visit the shop sometime again, real soon.

It was still raining like hell when we parted outside the Alamo and the sky was getting dark. To keep my new treasures from getting wet, I put the shiny black bag with *the Flames of Aladdin* and the Lucite wand under my jacket. I turned up my leather collar and walked as quickly as I could to the nearest subway. I couldn't wait to be seated on the train, heading back to Roslyn, trying to understand all that had been told to me. I felt like I was ten years older, maybe more.

# Patio of the Orange Trees

IN 1963, SHORTLY AFTER THE RESTORATION of Cordoba's
Mezquita, Dr. Julio Gayangos, chief of restoration, told this
story to Emilio Garcia Gomez, at the Café Horno de San Luis
on Calle del Corregidor.

SHADED FROM THE HEAT OF THE Andalusian sun, Modesto sat
on the ground, undoing the paper wrapper containing his
bread and olives. Alone among the stonemasons, he was not
going home for siesta. Although his uncle Luis's house was only
a few minutes' walk from the Mezquita, Modesto preferred to
take his rest in the Patio of the Orange Trees.

A breeze stirred the leaves overhead and the birds chirped as
he leaned his back against a tree and reflected on his last night
in Granada. He remembered coming home late to the rooms in
the Sacromonte caves that he shared with his friend Jaime. He
remembered reeling from the wild drinking and the gypsy
songs in the flamenco bars. He remembered hearing Jaime's
deep voice behind the beaded bedroom curtain, whispering in

low tones with a feminine voice. He remembered hesitating to part the beaded strands for fear of what he would find—his woman, Teresa, in bed with his roommate. He remembered pulling his belt knife out of its sheath and lunging at Jaime's chest. He remembered a neighbor, summoned by Teresa's screams, separating him from his bloody, unconscious friend. Modesto remembered waking the following day from a deep sleep, feeling no remorse at his attempt on Jaime's life. Despite his friend's refusal to press charges, he knew that if he stayed in Granada, he would try to kill Jaime again. Granada was no more than drunken nights now, without love, and a possible firing squad at the end. It was time to accept Uncle Luis's offer and get away.

Even before the knifing, Uncle Luis had been urging Modesto to leave his dissolute life in Granada and come to Cordoba. The Mezquita, the great mosque built by the Moors at the end of the eighth century, was celebrating its twelve hundredth anniversary with a massive restoration. As foreman of the stonemasons, Uncle Luis was in a position to secure a job for his only nephew. It would teach him a trade and earn him a steady income.

Seven months had passed since Modesto first accepted Uncle Luis's invitation, yet he still thought of his violent last night in Granada. Sitting in a tavern or his uncle's house, the image of Teresa's and Jaime's betrayal would enter his mind. His head would pound and his heart would ache. Only in the shade of the Patio of the Orange Trees could he recall the night as though it was occurring in a dream. Somehow the quiet order of the ancient grove made the night seem quiet and distant. It made the action take place in slow motion and the voices speak from the bottom of the sea. It made his heart still.

Relishing his peace, Modesto ate his bread and olives sheltered from the high sun. When his hunger was satisfied, and a full hour of siesta still remained, he picked up his mallet and chisel, walked past the fountains where the faithful once performed their ablutions, and entered the darkened Mezquita.

Wandering through the hundreds of marble and jasper columns, in perfect alignment with the rows of orange trees outside in the patio, Modesto's eyes became accustomed to the dim light. As they had during previous siestas, his legs, moved by a will of their own, led him to the mosque's domed mihrab. There, directed by a force he could not fathom, he set to work, chipping and cutting a large stone at the bottom of the niche. Though he had no idea what he had been carving over the past few weeks or why, Modesto took great pleasure in the beauty of the running, coursing lines he was creating on the surface of the stone. He knew the lines echoed in style the decorative script on the walls throughout the mosque. It was his hope that upon completion they would enhance the building's restoration.

That day, confident that his task was nearly done, Modesto worked feverishly, driving his chisel into the stone to release the last of the graceful, calligraphic designs trapped inside. At three o'clock, when the workers returned to their jobs, he was ready to show his handiwork to his uncle.

Modesto laid his mallet and chisels down and brushed the dust off the carving. He found Uncle Luis examining an outer wall on the southern side of the mosque with me. Awkwardly excusing himself, he told his uncle and I that he had something he wanted to show us in the prayer niche. The request was unusual and unexpected, but since it was made with such enthusiasm, we agreed to follow Modesto inside.

Immediately upon seeing the carving Uncle Luis became angry. He insisted that his nephew apologize to me for his desecration of the Mezquita, but I was not so quick to judge. Well acquainted with Maghribi script, I thought I recognized the lines of a poem in Modesto's carving. I ordered the area to be cordoned off and the inscription to be kept intact until it could be authenticated.

Three weeks later, after the stone had been scrutinized by Spain's leading Arabists, I received a letter with a translation of the lines Modesto had unknowingly carved in perfect Maghribi. The lines, written by Ibn Hazm, an eleventh-century Cordoban poet, who often composed his verses in the Patio of the Orange Trees, read as follows:

> *How I wish I could split my heart*
> *with a knife*
> *put you inside*
> *then close up my chest*
> *so that you could be in my heart*
> *and not in another's*
> *until the resurrection*
> *and the day of judgment.*
>
> *There you would stay while I lived*
> *and after my death*
>
> *you would remain buried deep in my heart*
> *in the darkness of the tomb.*\*

---

\*The poem by Ibn Hazm, is translated by Cola Frazen from the Spanish version of Emilio Garcia Gomez.

# The Birds of the Air

LONG AFTER THE TOWER BELLS CALLED the monks to their devotions, the ringing echoed in Brother Hugo's ears. It was a sensation unlike any he'd known in Paris, where even the bells of Notre Dame could be drowned in the city din: swine, sheep, and cattle led in noisy numbers through muddy streets, the swift gallop of horses, hawking merchants, whining beggars, the near-hysterical pitch of crowds on holy days, and above it all, the incessant verbal jousting of the men of the university—rowdy scholars and bands of students joking and drinking, quarreling and shouting in constant debate. In the college corridors, in the streets and taverns, Hugo walked among them, partaking of the intellectual feast. And sometimes in the middle of a labyrinthine argument, when lowering his voice to mark a fine point of logic, he'd regard their rapt, embattled faces and laugh uproariously.

All those discordant sounds were miles away from the shady arcades of the Abbey of Saint-Michel-de-Cuxa. There Brother Hugo walked in procession to chapel wondering when if ever he'd achieve the spiritual serenity he sought in monastic life. For try as he may, since he'd been at the abbey he couldn't keep his thoughts on God. The bells, the interludes of silence, the daily round of meals, the light at sunset, and the music of the psalms kept taking him back to the world he'd left behind—a world of heady ideas, with scholars embroiled in intellectual controversy, a turbulent world where philosophical war was waged between the claims of faith and reason, in the wake of recent translations into Latin of Aristotle's corpus.

Surrounded by his fellow monks with bowed, hooded heads before the chapel crucifix, Brother Hugo brooded on the atmosphere of intolerance and enmity that developed in his last days in Paris, when iron dogma and a perverse form of reason without heart fought for his allegiance. The collegial spirit was waning amid the bitter polemic. The joys of scholarship and instruction dimmed in the dark political wrangle. It was an insufferable atmosphere in which Hugo was torn between staying on at the university and leaving. To help him make a decision, he prayed to his patron saint for a sign.

One sleepless night it came. A fruit tree densely covered with white blossoms appeared before him at the foot of his bed. The vision grew large and he saw that it was birds, not flowers, covering the branches. One bird alighted from the tree and flew over a road winding out beyond his window into the distance. The flight drew him up from his bed with an incredible urge to follow the bird. From that moment, Brother Hugo knew he'd be leaving Paris.

THE ABBEY OF SAINT-MICHEL-DE-CUXA WAS A self-sufficient Benedictine enclave set in a quiet forest valley in the Pyrenees. Under the leadership of Abbot Olivier, its library had become celebrated throughout France. It was for that reason that Hugo chose the abbey as his refuge. In time, through the daily practice of his monastic duties, safe in an oasis of sanctity, he forgot the tumult of the world he'd left behind and turned his thoughts to God. Four hours a day he prayed to God the Father, the Son, and the Holy Ghost for the souls of the living and the dead, and never before did the mysteries of his faith seem more profound.

Because he'd been a university scholar, the Benedictine order required Hugo to perform the specific duties of teaching in the abbey school and copying manuscripts. But when duty allowed, at Olivier's urging he made use of the library's volumes of Plato, Augustine, and Boethius and wrote treatises on the Trinity and the Incarnation.

In spring and summer, when days were long, he tended the gardens and orchards. He felt closest there to God among the olive trees, palms, and grapevines lining the groves around the abbey; amid the iris, myrtle, and apple trees of the cloister; communing with the spiders, bees, and butterflies, and the larks, thrushes, and wrens whose continual singing was a melodious prayer.

Making use of his scientific learning, Brother Hugo filled notebooks with manifold observations of nature seen in the gardens and orchards. He described an apple from peel to core. He illustrated in detail the leaves of every tree and plant. He observed spiders spinning their webs and leaping on their prey, the honey making of bees, and the emergence of birds from eggs.

Olivier praised the scientific observations and welcomed the notebooks as an addition to the library. He believed, as Hugo did, that men could best understand their Creator once they understood in full the nature of his creations.

But Brother Hugo's happy, productive years at Saint-Michel-De-Cuxa came to an end. One chilly autumn night the abbot died in his sleep from the multiple woes of old age. Within weeks of Olivier's passing, the Benedictines appointed Ambrose of Arles to succeed him.

The new abbot, who arrived with an entourage more suitable to a knight than a clergyman, was a sanctimonious man who saw himself as a reformer. He was unread in the classics and philosophy. He had no sympathy for the new ideas coming from the cathedral schools and universities. And he believed that nature was the work of God and it wasn't man's place to inquire into the conundrums of the material world created by him.

To purge the abbey of his predecessor's "corruptions" the new abbot padlocked the library and banned the reading of anything other than Holy Scripture. And because Hugo, more than any of the monks, was to Ambrose the embodiment of Olivier's "decadent reign," he forbade him to teach and assigned him to twelve hours a day of manual labor.

Once again Brother Hugo found himself weighed down with melancholy, praying to his patron saint for a sign that would help him decide his future.

One sleepless night it came. A fruit tree densely covered with white blossoms appeared before him in his cell. The vision grew large and he saw that it was birds, and not flowers that covered the branches. One bird alighted from the tree and flew over a road winding out beyond his window into the distance. This vision drew him up from his bed with a great urge to follow the bird. From that moment he knew he'd be leaving the abbey.

EARLY CHRISTMAS MORNING WHILE THE ABBEY slept, Brother Hugo left the walls of Saint-Michel-De-Cuxa and set out on the pilgrim road to Compostela. He took nothing with him but his sandals, the gray and white robe he always wore, a wooden rosary, and a beggar's wallet. Though it was his original goal, it wasn't necessary that he reach the apostle James's shrine in western Spain. He simply wanted to further his distance from worldliness.

That winter the Pyrenees were particularly dangerous, but Hugo refused to be impeded by deep snow and the threat of avalanche. With each step he was retreating further and further into his solitude. Sustained by the generosity of the churches and hospices along the way, by spring he reached the swollen banks of the Aragon, a small tributary of the Ebro north of Saragossa.

It was nightfall as Brother Hugo stood on the eastern shore, wondering whether to wait until morning to make his crossing. As he stood and wondered, a little bird came and hovered over his head. The bird flew to the other side of the stream, and then back to Hugo. He made the same flight a second time. The third time Hugo followed him.

Having crossed the narrow but swollen tributary, Brother Hugo was exhausted and lay down on the shore. But the little bird wouldn't rest. He flew into the nearby woods, then back to Brother Hugo, perching on his head. He made the same flight a second time. The third time Hugo pulled himself up from the ground and followed him.

With a full moon overhead, the little bird and Brother Hugo went deep into the forest, coming to a stop in a clearing. There beneath a circular canopy of towering pines was an abandoned hut. The little bird flew in through the open doorway, and Hugo followed him. But for a crude table, a simple chair, and a straw pallet, the hut was empty.

Through a window on the rear wall Hugo saw a fruit tree densely covered with white blossoms. He stood closer to the window and saw that it was birds, not flowers, covering the branches—manifold birds whose singing was that of a heavenly choir. When he opened the window to better hear them, the birds suddenly flew into the hut. They perched on his head and shoulders and continued their madrigals. In the midst of their music, Hugo laughed uproariously.

# The White Lion

THE WAR HAD JUST ENDED WHEN Fabiano Fabrizi contracted scarlet fever. Years later, after his great talent as a film actor brought him international acclaim, he wrote about the illness and its aftermath in his autobiography, *La Vita Agrodolce*.

IT WAS DIFFICULT FOR EVERYONE. EVEN those like my parents who had been comfortable before the war were unable to find enough food for the table. Epidemics ran unchecked throughout Italy, scarlet fever being the one to come to Castello Fabrizi. The first to fall ill were the caretaker's children, Maria and Paolo, followed shortly by me. I remember an eternity of darkness in my bedroom and brief interruptions of light from the hallway when my parents or the doctor entered the room. They spoke in whispers—whispers and the pained eyes of my mother being an indication of the gravity of my illness. Of course, I was not told at the time, but the fever quickly claimed the lives of my playmates.

After Maria and Paolo's deaths, the concern of my parents for their only child was exacerbated. To encourage me to fight the disease, they offered to buy me a lion cub. I had a birthday due, my ninth, and the lion was promised as a gift, should I be well enough to receive it. Throughout the weeks prior to my birthday, I struggled with fever, sleep overtaking me most of the time. In rare moments of wakefulness, I recalled the promise made by my parents and thought that it had been made in a dream. They assured me that the promise was real, and little by little, the fever ran its course. I could sit in bed and play with soldiers, or draw pictures. By my birthday, standing, though still weak and confined to my room, I was out of danger.

True to their word, on the morning of my ninth birthday, my parents presented me with a baby lion. He was the most beautiful thing I had ever seen, white as snow, of a rare breed then being raised for domesticity. I named him Raphael because he was as perfect as a painting by the Renaissance master. With the help of the playful Raphael, I regained my strength and overcame the loss of Maria and Paolo. In the warm sunlight, in the walled garden behind our kitchen, we rolled over and over each other in the grass. Often my mother would join us. Blonde and fair, in tweed skirts, pastel sweaters, and a string of pearls, she was fond of sitting at the base of the lemon tree, with Raphael in her lap. She liked to open his jaw to see how large his teeth were getting. I believe that the idea to give me a lion cub was hers, more so than my father's, and that in order to afford Raphael, she sold her most cherished heirloom—a gold band set with diamonds.

In time the severity of conditions after the war lessened, and Raphael and I approached adolescence. I grew tall, and a sleek and muscular Raphael grew a mane. To celebrate our simultaneous coming of age, my father took us hunting. Along with my three uncles, we set out on a November morning. In 1949 the wooded hills of Umbria surrounding Castello Fabrizi were stocked with game, including wild boar. Raphael, who had never before been outside the walled kitchen garden, was ill at ease. He was startled at the slightest sound or movement. The frequent firing of my uncles' rifles at rabbits was especially agitating for him. When he could no longer tolerate the commotion, he bolted.

In the distance I could see him running, straight into the caretaker, who was up in the hills hunting for truffles with his donkey and dog. Surprised by the encounter, Raphael attacked the donkey, bringing him down with a bite to his jugular. In the ruckus, some of Raphael's flesh was torn off by the donkey, which kicked him in the shin. The wound was serious enough to require immediate attention and put an end to our hunting expedition. Amused by Raphael's choice for his first kill, my uncles cut off the donkey's head for a trophy. They tied the headless body to a pole, placed the pole on their shoulders, and my father, my uncles, Raphael, and I headed home. As we were leaving the woods, I turned around to look at the caretaker. He was down on his hands and knees, picking up the scraps of Raphael's flesh and eating them.

# The Passage of Juana Inez

JUANA INEZ'S MOTHER AND STEPFATHER WERE asleep in their bedroom down the hall, and her two older sisters were whispering in their beds in the room she shared with them. Outside the midday sun baked the clay roof tiles of the hacienda that clung to the mountainside, between the snows of Popocatepetl and the cane fields of the plain. The drowsy song of a sparrow was the only sound to invade the stillness, as the frail, fevered girl lay restless in her bed, thinking of the shadow being in her grandfather's library. When it first appeared a month ago, it startled her so much that she bolted from her studies and ran from the room. She was sure that the ghostly presence was one of the dangerous spirits common to the Mexican countryside. The Indian cook had warned her of spirits cheated by untimely deaths, which amused themselves by wreaking havoc on the living. But since the initial, frightening encounter, Juana Inez had come to feel a protective closeness whenever the shadow being visited her in the library, and over time, she became convinced that the spirit was her late grandfather, as yet unable to part from his beloved books.

The heavy summer heat pressed around her and the whispering of her fat sisters continued. To blot out the discomfort and annoyance, Juana Inez itemized the clues that led her to believe that the shadow and her grandfather were one and the same.

First, there were the jumping books in the section of the library devoted to natural sciences. When he was alive, Pedro Ramirez had shown a vigorous curiosity for all disciplines, and just prior to his death, his intellectual attention was focused on a study of the natural world, in particular the songbirds of his adopted Mexico. Against the objections of Juana Inez's mother, he spent lavishly on beautifully illustrated volumes of birds that took months to arrive by ship from Spain. Now some of those volumes were becoming dislodged from the shelves, as though plucked by cloud fingers, unable to hold them for more than a moment.

There was the ornately carved bookrest that turned up on the library table after the spirit's first visit. Since no one in the household made use of the library other than Juana Inez, the appearance of the bookrest was highly unusual, and the young girl suspected her grandfather's handiwork.

After all, he'd often promised to craft such a stand for his favorite granddaughter to further enhance the pleasure of her studies.

The falling songbird books. The bookrest, but most of all the absence of loneliness made Juana Inez feel that a protective spirit was watching her.

In a family consumed with pedestrian interests, Pedro Ramirez had been the only one with whom Juana Inez could identify. Along with his cleverness, his skill in argument, and his imagination, she shared his angular frame, strong features, and pale skin. He'd been her champion, the only one to encourage her dreaming and investigation of the world.

When he died, she had felt so lonely and despondent. She

cut her hair, she began to dress like a boy, and she begged her mother to send her away to school. Her mother flatly refused. Young girls in Mexico, no matter how short their hair or how they dressed, were not sent to school. To console herself, Juana Inez spent all of her days in the library, studying and reading with greater urgency than ever before.

She applied herself to the difficult task of learning Latin. After weeks of study, when she still hadn't mastered the language, she cut off more of her hair. She stopped eating cheese, her favorite food, because she heard that it could make a person slow-witted. She stopped eating beef, and then chicken, and refused all meals other than breakfast, which she ate in the kitchen in the company of the Indian cook. Thin to begin with, her mother was concerned that she was disappearing. To punish her for her self-enforced starvation and drastic appearance, Juana Inez's mother forbade her access to the library. The doors were locked and the servants were given orders never to enter the room again. "Let it rot," Juana Inez's mother said. "It's been good for nothing but the squandering of the family's fortune on useless books."

Juana Inez was made to suffer again through three meals a day with her gross family, but now when she was given permission to leave the table, she went out behind the house and vomited her food. Before long she found a way to get into the library and close the doors behind her by inserting a small piece of iron into the locks. During siestas, or late at night, while her family slept the deep sleep of the dull and overfed, she made her way, undetected, to her special place.

She resumed her study of Latin, which at first went slowly, until the shadow came. Then, almost instantaneously, what had seemed difficult and hard to understand became knowledge she could acquire with ease. She no longer felt lonely. She felt energized and inspired. She broadened her course of study to investigate ancient history, mythology, and poetry. And sometimes, lost in a book propped on the ornate bookrest, she felt a gentle stroke on her cheek.

Finally, after a stretch that seemed to last for hours, Juana Inez heard the snores of her sisters. Weak as she was, she pulled herself up from her bed and slipped out of the room. She tiptoed down the hall, catching a glimpse of her mother's large breasts, rising and falling under her husband's heavy arm. Making her way to the door leading to the courtyard, she was dizzy and had to lean on the walls for support. Like the ghost of a boy, with her cropped hair and her grandfather's cotton nightshirt trailing behind her, she glided under the shaded arcade to the north wing of the house. She undid the locks, and with all the strength she could muster, she pushed the thick doors open and entered the library.

Amid the dust, the darkness, and the cobwebs she was happy to be surrounded by the volumes telling of the once glorious cities of Petra and Alexandria, of camel caravans over bleached desert sands, and barges on the Nile, laden with leopard skins and trunks of sub-Saharan pachyderms. She looked lovingly at the many volumes devoted to the Spain of her ancestors, the gypsy caves above the Alhambra, the gold of the Aztecs, paving the streets of Seville, monasteries high in the Pyrenees, and the University of Salamanca, where she longed to study. Here were the volumes that made real to her the violent myths of the Greeks, played out among the stars, and the books by her beloved poets, so honored by divine favor that they stirred her soul.

Juana Inez scanned the room for the wispy pillar of smoke. It wasn't there, but she knew from experience that it might appear at any moment. Having been advised by the Indian cook that spirits preferred darkness, she opened the shutters just wide enough to allow a dim reading light into the room. Then she sat down to her studies.

In front of an open volume of Virgil on the ornate book rest, she noticed a large green volume that hadn't been there the previous day. It was *Vireos of Cozumal, Veracruz and the Yucatan*, her grandfather's favorite songbird book. The nearness of it filled her with joy and heightened her readiness for the wanderings of Aeneas.

As she read, Juana Inez began to feel the weight of an enormous tiredness overcome her, and try as she may, her efforts to resist it were futile. The tiredness must be from lack of sleep, she thought, or her meager daily sustenance of a cup of Indian herb tea. Her eyes started to lose focus on the words in front of her, and took rest in the play of light filtering into the room. Delicate shadows cast by the leaves and branches of the eucalyptus tree outside moved across the ceiling, over the stacked shelves, and the open pages of Virgil, coalescing into a single, smoky pillar, an almost indiscernible vacuum of light that settled into a chair across from her. As it did so, the cover of the songbird book opened, and the pages began to turn.

In her half-conscious state, the little girl's excitement made her body shake. To steady herself, she took hold of either side of the book rest. She felt her hands grasp the wood, but she couldn't see her hands, or her forearms. The volume of Virgil and the songbird book started to fade and her head felt like a stone, falling. A soft blanket of eternal rest was wrapping around her. But before it completely engulfed her, Juana Inez saw an old wrinkled hand reach out and place itself where her hand had been.

After the passage of Juana Inez, the authorities searched the hacienda and the surrounding countryside for her, but not a trace was found. The common consensus was that she had run away, but an investigation of every convent and boarding school in the province revealed nothing. The Indian cook suggested that the girl might be hiding in the library, but since the library had been shut for months and its doors remained locked, Juana Inez's mother refused to consider the possibility. Only when the cook's suggestion became an annoying plea did Juana Inez's mother relent.

Aside from the dust and the cobwebs, which she expected, Juana Inez's mother was surprised to find the room in such disarray. Books were fallen from the shelves, volumes were open on the table, and the shutters were parted. In a chair in front of an ornate book rest, which she vaguely recalled having seen in an unfinished state in her father's workshop, she found one of Pedro Ramirez's nightshirts. Angered by what she assumed was the servants' failure to straighten up the library before it was permanently closed, she grabbed the nightshirt and stormed into the kitchen.

At the sight of the old white shirt, the Indian cook let out a scream and began to sob. It was her fault, she said, that Juana Inez had disappeared. She knew of the long, secret hours the girl was spending in the library, wearing her grandfather's nightshirt. It was she who had encouraged Juana Inez to wear the shirt and to believe that the shadow being who visited her in the library was her grandfather. She had instructed the eager girl in the ways of Indian magic and had prepared a daily tea for her of Indian herbs. It was the tea that Indians drank when they wished to leave their bodies.

The cook's words infuriated Juana Inez's mother. There was no such thing as magic, she said, and no daughter of hers would ever be involved in anything so foolish. If the cook expected to keep her job in a Christian household, she had best leave her superstitions at the door. People didn't evaporate into thin air, she said. In God's universe, there was a practical explanation for her daughter's disappearance.

To prove her point, Juana Inez's mother requested the authorities to expand the perimeters of their search. Every remote mountain ridge, cave, or isolated stream that had previously been ignored was scrutinized. Every sighting, in every distant village, of a girl fitting Juan Inez's description, was examined She had the library books and furniture, and the old nightshirt burned in a heap, as far away from the hacienda as possible. The local padre gave the room a fresh blessing, and less than a year after the passage, the room was converted into a sporting room. Guns and rifles were placed in glass cases where the bookshelves had been and the heads of deer and jaguars were mounted above them.

# Autumn Melancholy

CATHERINE DE MONTCHENSI WAS A YOUNG Occitanian wife in the age of *l'amour courtois* and the jeweled sunburst on the Virgin's breast. The age of hell's bedlam—*janua diaboli*—the earthly woman awakened to her nature. She had been betrothed in childhood to an older man, a marriage arranged by her father in the interests of land—and at the age of thirteen, she left her home in Pau to enter her husband's castle in Toulouse. Animated by a high spirit, Catherine quickly mastered the courtly conventions: hawking, playing chess, learning letters, singing, and playing musical instruments. But in spite of these amusements, her time passed dismally. For although her husband provided her with every luxury, she resented her conjugal subjection, and longed for a love that was freely sought and freely given.

One day as she was training her goshawk by the river, Catherine encountered Arnaut Vidal, engaged in the composition of a chanson. So strong was her attraction for the troubadour that she released her hawk, letting it fly from her wrist.

And the jongleur, feeling the same magnetic pull, dropped the rebec in midsong. That afternoon they began an idyll, fearlessly following their heart's urges, making love in a grotto beyond the castle's walls. After three months of clandestine meetings, Catherine's husband interrupted the romance. He had grown suspicious of his young wife and followed her into the fields. Enraged by his cuckolding, he reacted violently. Catherine was brought back to the castle, where she was fitted with an iron girdle of chastity. And the lord's hired men chased Arnaut to the edge of the fiefdom, where he was brutally castrated. The tragedy led Catherine to take up a veil of sorrow in a convent, while Arnaut found a refuge in monasticism.

Five hundred years after the forceful separation, the remains of Catherine de Montchensi were discovered beneath the abbey in Saint-Guilhem-le-Deserte, along with a box containing chansons by Arnaut Vidal. The exquisite lyrics praised the young wife for her beauty and refinement. They spoke of the ennobling quality of love and described woman as the ladder on which to climb to heaven. As soon as the bones were found, they were brought to the square in Pau, where a monument—which still stands today, as white as a Pyrenean snowdrift—was erected. The monument depicts a beautiful female figure enveloped in loose drapery, reclining on a sarcophagus. The face of the figure wears a melancholic expression and the body's posture suggests a convalescent, eternally recovering from a sickness of the heart. Throughout the centuries, the statue was perceived by its beholders to be a saint of love. People brought flowers and placed them at its base. There they knelt and prayed for an intercession in their love lives.

Two hundred years after Catherine de Montchensi's remains were discovered, the bones of Arnaut Vidal were unearthed beneath the monastery in Limoges, along with a box containing letters from Catherine. The letters reminded the troubadour of how much like an altar was the bed of consummation with his lady, and they compared the nourishment of the spiritual fire of erotic love to the nourishment that the lover of God received from the bread and wine of the Eucharist. As soon as Arnaut's remains were found, they were brought to Pau and laid beside Catherine in a marble reclining naked youth, with a face that wore an archaic smile. On the day of its unveiling, a great ceremony was held in the square. Dignitaries came from as far away as Paris. An orchestra played the overture to Wagner's *Tristan und Isolde.* As the music reached its rapturous peak, the canvas cloth covering the statue was removed, revealing the lovers, side by side, with the inscription *"conjugium in aeternum"* chiseled into the stone of their common plinth.

On the day following the ceremony, the strange events began. The first thing noticed was the altered expression on Catherine's face. Gone was her melancholic expression. It had been replaced with an archaic smile. And the folds of drapery covering her body had disappeared. Even more startling was the sudden, powerful pull one felt on approaching the statues. It was as though they were imbued with magnetism. Many were frightened by the changes. But many more realized that a miracle had occurred; and within days of the coming together of the young wife and the troubadour, a cult of love was initiated.

People in love, and people seeking love, came to the square with flowers. They stood at the base of the monuments, where the aura was so intense that one became endowed with the virtues of the lovers on the sarcophagi. Worshippers held candlelight vigils and slept at the feet of the statues, hoping that as they slept the spirits of Catherine and Arnaut would enter their bodies. Soon word of the miracle spread throughout the country. Visitors arrived by train from all over the continent. The existing hotels filled to capacity and new ones had to be built to accommodate the continuous stream of pilgrims.

Additional priests were needed in Pau to meet the demand for marriages and the town swelled with intoxicated wedding guests reluctant to go home. Couples wishing to conceive a child started making love at night at the base of the statues. Soon couples wishing to insure their union joined them. Strangers sought each other out during the day, waiting until nightfall to make love. Eventually the cultists grew too impatient to wait for nightfall and started making love during the day. In broad daylight, the square was strewn with naked bodies, orgies, and drunkenness. The fevered pitch grew, until one day, at the height of the frenzy, someone castrated the statue of Arnaut Vidal. The same person broke open the sarcophagus and made away with Arnaut's bones.

The mutilation had an immediately sobering effect. The magnetic aura surrounding the statues ceased and the naked revelers filed out of the square. It was only after the last of the pilgrims were gone and the square returned to quiet that one noticed the statue of Catherine de Monchensi. Gone was her smile. It had been replaced with a melancholic gaze. And the posture of her body, beneath the folds of drapery, suggested the languor of a convalescent.

# Fire Worshippers

*As told to Viola Cooper, professor of Oriental Studies, London University, at the Parsee Temple, Madras, India, 1937*

OUTSIDE THE MONSOON RAINS COME DOWN but the fire is safe. The shadows of the flames dance on the walls. It's quiet here and dry. The roof of every house leaks. But the temple tiles are sealed. The fire burns. The flames dance and cast a glow— orange in the rain, yellow when the sun pours through the windows, distant-planet red at night.

The fire first came to the people when a piece of star broke off and fell to Earth. One woman was awake to witness the sliver slice through the darkness. It landed on the sand where she stood—a small rock with spokes radiating from the core like petals of a brilliant flower. The burning piece was so hot it singed the hair on her legs. She watched the petals jump from the rock to a bush to a thorn tree, which was dressed with the light of a thousand stars. That night the woman's excited cries alerted the people. They came and stood in awe of the fire.

They gave it a name worthy of its wonder. Scrub brush was gathered to keep the piece of burning star alive and where it fell the first altar was erected.

The coming of fire changed everything. The people could light the interior of their tents at night and cook their food. They began to shine more brightly, feeling at one with the sand, the sky, the sun, and the stars. The fire brought an elevation of spirit and sharpness of mind not previously experienced.

Inspired, the people invented metallurgy and made lanterns and bowls for fire altars. They invented an alphabet to record theories on the nature and origins of fire. Scholars wrote books addressing questions aroused by the arrival of the fragment of star: Was fire an embodiment of the divine? Why had it chosen such a form? What was fire made of? Was it the soul of the sun glimmering through pinholes in the dark? Had it originated in the distant red planet? Was it a strand of a high ranking seraph's hair cut off in battle? Had it been sent from camps in the high desert? Why were certain spices, gums, and perfumed woods its favorite offerings? Why did it favor thorn trees? Were lions, horses, and eagles made of fire?

So many books were written a library had to be built. For its location a valley in the steep foothills of the holy mountains was chosen. Scholars turned their backs on desert life and made a permanent camp around the library. The first temple, a building even larger and more beautiful than the library, was built for the burning fragment of star. In time the encampment grew into a city.

To bring in each New Year, a Festival of Fire was held in the city. People came in great numbers from the desert. They set up tents and stayed a fortnight. They dressed in white—the color at the tips of flames before they disappear into the air. During the day they fasted and prayed. They made offerings of incense and red petals in the temple. They visited the library to hear

the latest investigations of the scholars. At night they celebrated. They visited each other's tents and ate elaborate feasts.
On the last day the women torched thorn-tree branches in the
burning fragment and captured the flames in lanterns to bring
back to the desert.

One year when the people were assembled for the festival,
strangers rode into the city. They shouted at the people from
high mounts. They said the divine was invisible and only an
ignorant people would worship fire. They stomped their boots
on the campfires outside the people's tents, but the flames
resisted. They ordered the people to throw buckets on their
fires, but the people refused. The strangers attempted to storm
the temple, but the people created a barricade that held firm. In
fury the strangers ransacked the library.

After a day of bullying, the strangers were exhausted. The
people cleverly blew the thick smoke of poppy gum into their
faces and put them to sleep. That horrible day all the books in
the library were destroyed. Many people were injured, but no
one was killed. The people knew the strangers would eventually wake up. They also knew their wit was no match for the
ferocity and numbers of the horsemen. So they broke camp.
They tied their belongings to the backs of their camels. They
retrieved the burning piece of star from the temple. They
encased it in a brass lantern to protect it from the wind and
they left the city.

Never stopping, they headed east across rivers and mountains. The journey was difficult. For those who had become
accustomed to life in the city, it was wrought with hardship.
The scholars, especially, did not fare well. Only the hardiest
nomadic people made it to the final destination, and upon
arrival, more than half of them succumbed to diseases bred by
tropical heat and humidity.

Now the monsoon rains come down and the desert is a distant
longing in our hearts. Still we do our best to practice the old

ways. Though this land is impoverished, we are safe. The local people worship strange gods, but they are agreeable. They leave us alone. We've kept our language. We've built a temple and a temple school. In recent years the school has even produced a few scholars, and after many generations in this hot, wet place, we're building our first library.

In three months' time we will have the Festival of Fire. Everyone will dress in white. Each family will come to the temple with a lantern. From the burning piece of star the women will take a flame. They will put it in their lanterns to protect it from the rain. Then they will return to their homes with fresh bundles of thorn trees and start the hearth fires for the New Year.

As a descendant of the woman at whose feet the first fire fell, it is my responsibility to gather the fresh supply of thorn-tree branches for this year's festival. Without thorn-tree branches the New Year can't begin. To collect the branches it's necessary to travel to the only region where they grow—the region of the holy mountains outside the old city. Since the people fled, the city and the surrounding lands have been occupied by the angry worshippers of an invisible deity. They have given the city a name of their choosing. To us it is an unspeakable name.

Tradition calls for me to make the journey with a band of women. It is a dangerous undertaking over a harsh terrain to which the people are no longer accustomed. Some have left not to return. For those who make it to the region, their lives depend on not being detected. Before we leave we will make offerings of spices, gums, and perfumed woods. We shall pray that the fire in its benevolence accepts our offerings and ensures our safety.

# The Astronomer

AT A CARAVANSARY IN KHURASAN, BENEDETTO Cantari encountered an indigent Persian nobleman. Dressed in a soiled turban and threadbare silken coat, the nobleman spent his days squatting silently in the arched entranceway with a begging bowl and an embroidered satchel over his shoulder. At night he bought bread and hashish with the few coins given him and walked out into the desert. Benedetto watched the nobleman with growing fascination throughout his stay at the caravansary, and the night before he and his caravan were to resume their journey back to Venice from Cathay, he followed the solitary figure.

They walked for an hour before Benedetto called out to the Persian, who then encouraged Benedetto to join him on his blanket in a small oasis marked by a tiny pool and a grove of trees. Once they were seated, the nobleman lit his hashish pipe and inhaled the smoke in long, luxurious drafts. Soon the sad dignity, that characterized his countenance was replaced with an expression of boyish excitement, and the blank pools of his eyes mirrored the brilliance of the night sky. Benedetto was anxious to know more about the man, unlike anyone he had come across during his travels, so he prodded him with questions. In time, inspired by the hashish and the Venetian's sympathetic curiosity, the nobleman told his story.

His name was Qutb al-Din al Fazari. He was born a nomad and developed his obsession with the night sky as a child. As a young man he was apprenticed to an astronomer in Maraghah. His exceptional observations won him the favor of Husayn Khan, who appointed him astronomer to the court. The Mongol ruler was so pleased with Qutb al-Din's ability to divine the future that he rewarded him with an observatory. Equipped with a revolving dome, astrolabes, armillary, quadrants, nocturnals, celestial globes, and a library, the new observatory easily excelled those in Cairo and Damascus. With twelve assistants to help him, Qutb al-Din spent many years casting horoscopes, devising calendars, testing mathematical tables, and measuring the distances between the heavenly bodies.

His finest achievement came in his fortieth year, when sparing neither labor nor expense, Husayn Khan sponsored al-Din's construction of an optic tube. With the aid of the tube, he discovered myriads of unknown stars. To the nine stars in the belt and sword of Orion, he added eighty, and to the seven in the Pleiades, thirty-six more were detected. His great astronomical compendium, *The Book of Millions*, which included a treatise on the optic tube, had just been completed when misfortune occurred. The rivalry between Husayan Khan and his younger brother, Ahmed, which had been the source of endless court intrigue, finally came to a head when Ahmed's followers killed the Persian's patron.

Ahmed, the new Ilkhan, was a zealot who felt the sciences posed a threat to his religious beliefs. Deeply disturbed by the invention of a glass that detected invisible stars, Ahmed ordered the destruction of the observatory and the execution of the astronomer. Aided by Husayan's former administrator, Qutb al-Din al Fazari fled Maraghah with the sole copy of *The Book of Millions* and whatever necessities his camel bags would hold. He traveled east, exchanging his possessions for food and shelter along the way. When he arrived at the caravansary in Khurasan his only possessions were *The Book of Millions*, in his embroidered satchel and his camel. He sold the camel, ensuring his begging spot indefinitely.

Benedetto asked if he could see *The Book of Millions*. Al-Din carefully removed the thick volume it from his satchel. The brown leather cover was smooth with age, but when opened, the illuminated interior glowed like a marriage of the moon and sun, so pristine was the white of the pages, so shining the gold of the elaborate embellishments. The whole was a work of art, including the elegant lines of Farsi in Persian script and the embossed borders. Benedetto couldn't read the words, but he sensed the value of the knowledge they contained.

BENEDETTO CANTARI WATCHED AS QUTB-AL-DIN REFILLED his pipe. Having heard the remarkable story of his past, the Venetian asked the astronomer about his plans for the future. Qutb-al-Din drew deeply on his pipe and exhaled. He said he was no longer concerned with continuing on to Samarkand or Kabul in search of a new patron. The longer he stayed at the caravansary, the more his ties with the world were being loosened. Benedetto wondered why, if that were the case, al-Din still held on to his illuminated treatise. The astronomer's answer surprised the Venetian. He said he had been waiting for someone to arrive at the caravansary, someone with whom he could entrust his knowledge. He asked him to take it with him in the morning when he resumed his journey. He told Benedetto to take it all the way to Venice, have it translated and presented to a wide and enlightened audience. Cantari promised to do so. He said that of all the treasures he was bringing back from Asia, nothing would surpass *The Book of Millions*.

The Persian thanked the Venetian and drew again on his pipe. With the parting of his book, he said his ties to the world he had once known were now completely loosened. He hadn't felt so free or content since he was a child. Once again, he could observe the sky's marvels as the nomads did. At night on the vast plain of Khurasan, he could look into the vault of the heavens. All the invisible stars he had once observed with his optic tube were now visible to his naked eyes with the assist of the mud-brown agent of hashish.

# Pictures at an Exhibition

*for Michael*

"THE RAPTURE OF THE DIONYSIAN STATE, with its annihilation of
the ordinary bounds and limits of existence, contains an ele-
ment in which all personal experiences of the past become
immersed. This chasm of oblivion separates the worlds of
everyday reality and of Dionysian reality. And as soon as
everyday reality re-enters consciousness, it is experienced with
nausea. . ." I'm reading to Michael from a 1911, Moroccan-blue,
leatherbound British edition of Nietzsche's *The Birth of Tragedy:
Out of the Spirit of Music*. It's a bright, cold, early Sunday afternoon in February and we're very stoned, riding uptown in a
cab, headed for the Rothko retrospective at the Guggenheim.

"'The chasm of oblivion. . .' Isn't this a beautiful little book?
I found it yesterday in front of one of the townhouses, across
the street from my building. I think an old resident must have
passed away and his relatives placed his personal effects,
including his library, on the curb to be collected with the trash.

Most of the books weren't interesting, but this one caught my eye with its Moroccan-blue cover. I put it in my pocket and walked away, not knowing it was *The Birth of Tragedy*."

On Sixth Avenue, there's very little traffic because it's Sunday, a very cold Sunday. The cab turns east on Central Park South, bringing into view the bare tops of the trees in Central Park, the St. Moritz, Trader Vic's, the Plaza and the fountain, stilled. On to Madison.

"You know, *The Birth of Tragedy* was one of Rothko's favorite books."

"Really?"

"Oh, yes," Michael says. "Rothko felt a great affinity for Nietzsche's romantic ideas of art as a healing sorceress who alone could transform the absurdity of existence into something livable—the sublime as a means of blocking out the horrible. It's an idea shared by many artists who feel uneasiness in the world. For Nietzsche, music was the most healing of the arts. He emphasized the dithyrambic chorus in Dionysian tragedy, which leads the listener back to the very heart of nature—back to a direct contact with knowledge unknown to reason. Like Nietzsche, Rothko craved the transport music could provide. There are stories of him lying on the grass in Vermont, or on a sofa in a Roman apartment, listening with rapt attention to *Don Giovanni*—oblivious to the world!"

The cab goes up Madison to Eightieth Street, and then turns west. Getting out at Fifth, our eyes are stroked by Frank Lloyd Wright's organic confection sitting on its base like a futuristic wedding cake. The museum's just opened and the line leading into the exhibition isn't long. Within minutes we're inside. I feel a sudden rush of excitement, once we pass the admissions desk. Standing under the domed skylight, it's so great to feel the enormity of the Guggenheim's open interior flooded with light. My excitement is heightened by glimpses, here and there, of the brilliant orange and red rectangles on the spiraling ramps above.

We took the elevator up ninety-two feet above the ground floor, where the winding, vertiginous descent begins. At the beginning, small, somber landscapes. Thick, muddy paint. Rothko's subway platform paintings with elongated figures waiting for trains that never arrive. Michael, true art scholar that he is, wants to linger over every bit of printed information on the walls, every early oil, watercolor and gouache. But I'm impatient. I want the classics. The big, stacked rectangles. The sublime rectangles. The otherworldly rectangles on the ramps ahead. I can't wait to get to them. Even the surreal, dancing forms on the pale gray and ochre beaches from the forties aren't enough to hold my interest. So I slip away, leaving Michael engaged in a concentrated study of *Slow Swirl at the Edge of the Sea*.

I walk quickly, avoiding the outer edge of the ramp and the sheer drop beyond it. Walking quickly, the floor sloping, past paintings with patches of color. Rose, red, yellow. Rectangles breaking out of their shells with tiny egg teeth. Orange, blue, sienna patches of color in flux, so loosely painted, with so much of the feel of watercolor. Walking quickly, almost hearing the Debussy and Ravel that Rothko must have played in the studio while he worked on these preliminaries to the classics. Red, red, red. In front of the last precursory painting, I pause to take in all of its sanguinary passion, broken by the stained blue outline of a red rectangle, at the core. Faster, faster. My heart racing because I know what's waiting around the bend.

*Violet, Black, Orange, Yellow on White and Red*, 1949. The age of wonder begins! And I'm immersed in it. The thrilling, pulsating, sensuous color. The light radiating through the transparent layers of paint. The light that issues from the depths of the enormous canvases, causing haloes and nimbuses around the blurry, shimmering edges of the rectangles, floating effortlessly.

There's just so much to take in. So much unbelievable color. So much light. So much vibration. So much, that if I close my eyes, I'm blinded by throbbing auras of red, orange, yellow, pink, and I start to feel dizzy. From what? The encounter of masterpiece after masterpiece? The strong grass we smoked before coming uptown? The spiraling, unsettling design of the Guggenheim? Around me, the museum starts to spin. The paintings start to sway. And I'm standing in a painting, standing in a doorway, leading to another world. I step back to the low wall running along the outer edge of the ramp, hoping to steady myself. But the floor beneath me starts to move. I turn my back on the paintings, but the sight of the open space in the center of the museum makes me tremble. I feel as though a disembodied force, a giant sucking force, is about to pull me over the side of the wall, making me fall, fall, fall to my death in the little blue sliver of a pool on the ground floor. To reassure myself, and catch my breath, I turn around and face the paintings again. I squat down and huddle against the base of the ramp wall. But a premonition of the floor giving way beneath me sends me running off the ramp, into one of the galleries housing part of the museum's permanent collection.

Soft, calm, clear, the tranquilizing violins of Tchaikovsky's *Serenade for Strings in C* envelop me as I enter. Emanating from the labyrinthine heart of the gallery, the music's mesmerizing effect draws me toward its source. Buoyed by melody, past the exposed wall ordinarily displaying Kandinsky, Leger, Mondrian, Klee, and Delaunay, I lightly step on the level floor. The smell of turpentine permeates the air, and I gather that the gallery's being painted, though there's no evidence to lead me to that conclusion. No buckets, no brushes, no ladders, no hanging sheets of plastic, no freshly painted wall covering the shadowy outlines of absent pictures.

The music grows louder and louder. I turn yet another corner into an incredibly large, bright room where the music's source, an audio cassette player, sits on a wooden stool, bouncing from the volume. As often as I've visited this gallery in the past, I know I've never been in this room. Its square footage and high, sky-lit ceiling has more of the atmosphere of a studio than a museum gallery. Three of the room's walls are bare, but on the wall facing me, a mural-sized painting hovers in space, detached and freed of a frame. Unlike anything I've ever seen, the painting actually seems to breathe. A vital entity. Constable's clouds come to life. Two vaguely defined, warm, white rectangles, touch with the faintest gold, blue and rose of a Turner sky. The palest summer sunlight ground hugs and separates the rectangles.

As I'm looking at this spectacular landscape, a ghostlike figure made of the same substance as the painting steps out from behind the wall. Dressed in shades of gray—a dark gray overcoat, charcoal gray suede shoes, gray trousers, and gray-on-gray pinstriped shirt—he's wiping paint from his hands with a soiled handkerchief. After a moment, he looks up from the business of cleaning his hands, and I realize it's Rothko. There he is with his balding pate, his gray hair, his sad eyes, the pale plastic frames of his glasses, and the ever-present cigarette in his mouth. Our eyes meet. He walks over to the cassette recorder and lowers the volume. "I'm glad you came," he says. "I have something for you." He reaches into his coat pocket and takes out what appears to be a small pouch. "I really have no use for these anymore. I thought you might like them."

With all the strength I can muster, I walk over to Rothko and take the object from his hand. It's a black velvet pouch holding marbles made of precious and semiprecious stones. I empty some of the marbles into my hand. Dazzling jewels, in all the colors of the spectrum. Ruby, sapphire, topaz, emerald, amethyst, and fire-opal marbles. They're magnificent.

I'm at a total loss as to how to thank him when I remember the Moroccan-blue copy of *The Birth of Tragedy* in my pocket. "Here,"

I say, extending my hand, "I have something for you, too." Rothko takes the book and reads the title with an expression of disbelief. He caresses the leather covers and looks up at me with the sweetest smile. We stand locked in comfortable silence, our eyes fixed on each other. Then little by little, Rothko begins to fade away, until he's completely gone, and his landscape is gone as well.

I tuck the velvet pouch into my pocket and slowly, reluctantly make my way back to the outer ramp. Now the retrospective is mobbed with people. My stomach is upset and I feel overwhelmed from the contact with so many bodies. In front of a maroon and red masterpiece, I reunite with Michael.

"Where have you been?"

"Looking at paintings."

"Did you already go to the bottom of the ramp and then turn around?"

"No, I was looking at the paintings from the fifties," I lie.

"Well, I was just there, and I didn't see you."

Because it's become impossible to stand back and look at anything without having to crane our necks over and around dozens of heads, Michael and I don't linger over Rothko's subdued palette paintings of the sixties, even though they're some of my favorites. Instead we walk past the olive greens and purples and on to Rothko's "endgame."

The last paintings. The blacks. The grays. The browns and blues. The bleak glimpses of eternity. Always the horizontal. Always the dark, foreboding emptiness in the top half of the canvas. Huge views of a lunar surface? Views from the edge of a desert at night? Views through a window on a despairing soul? The work of a man preparing for death? I don't know. All I know is that I find these paintings as to be as awesome as the early rectangles. And without the warm, sensuous, pulsating colors, they're a soothing, fitting denouement.

Outside the Guggenheim, Michael and I get lucky and grab a cab right away.

"It was great, wasn't it?"

"Oh, unbelievable!"

"We'll have to go back. We can go back next Sunday and go straight to the sixties paintings."

"Yeah, that would be great," I say. Even though we're out of the museum, my stomach is churning, my head feels woozy, and my mind is stunned. I sit back in the cab and try to enjoy the ride down Fifth Avenue, ordinarily one of my favorite rides.

"Should we get something to eat?"

"I don't know. I'm feeling out of sorts from the crush of the crowds and all that body heat."

"Okay. We'll wait and see how you feel when we get to your apartment."

How can it be that I actually met Rothko?

"Let me see *The Birth of Tragedy*," Michael says. "There's a section near the beginning where Nietzsche talks about music being the highest degree of universal language—obviously the degree Rothko was trying to achieve with paint."

"I don't have it anymore," I say, fondling the velvet pouch in my pocket.

"What do you mean you don't have it anymore?"

"I left it behind in the museum."

"How could you leave it behind in the museum?"

"Michael, this is going to sound crazy, but . . ."

# Lake of the Buddhas

IN HER FIFTEENTH YEAR, SINCA WAS chosen to be the bride of the Water Spirit. The Great Python, living in a submarine palace under the Mahaweli Ganga, was tired of his old wife, who bore him only female offspring.

The moon glowed in the fullness of the month of the White Monkey, when Sinca's attendants rubbed her with snake oil and dressed her in snakeskins. They draped her with necklaces, bracelets, and anklets made of egg teeth. As a token of love from the Water Spirit, the Serpent Chief brought her a temple viper with a ruby in its mouth. Carrying the viper, Sinca walked in procession to the riverbank.

Beside the Mahaweli Ganga, in all her finery, Sinca presided over the drowning of the Water Spirit's old wife and daughters. She kissed the head of a living cobra and fed it a drop of her finger's blood. She drank wine and ate the organs of a snake to ensure her fertility. She crawled through a tunnel formed by the spread legs of her male worshippers, and one by one, she mated with the serpent priests.

At the end of the night, Sinca fell asleep on the warm sand of the riverbank and dreamed of the Great Python rising to the surface of a lake on a lotus blossom. The blossom drifted to the far side of the lake, where the Great Python stepped out of the blossom and onto the shore, in the form of a beautiful young man. The young man sat on the shore and spoke: "The perfume of virtue travels against the wind and reaches to the ends of the world. Arise, and walk on the middle path. Lift yourself up, as an elephant lifts himself from a muddy swamp." The young man walked around the lake, stopping at five different locations to speak the same words. Then he disappeared into the sky on a flowery cloud.

When Sinca awoke it was dark, and a light rain was falling on the naked bodies beside the river. She removed her heavy snakeskins and her jewelry and found a coarse cloth with which to cover herself. She lit a torch, to keep the wild animals at a distance, and set out into the jungle.

For a year Sinca wandered the forests, living on the fruits and herbs she found. When the next White Monkey moon arrived, she came upon a secluded lake, surrounded by five colossal, bronze statues. The statues were exact replicas of the beautiful young man as he sat on the shore and spoke in her dream. A pleasant sound issued from the water, filling her with gladness and calm. At once Sinca knew that to tend the shrine was her calling. She picked up a sharp object and cut off the ends of her hair. And when she was satisfied with her appearance, she began to gather garlands of sandalwood, rosebay, and jasmine to place in the laps of the statues.

# ABOUT THE AUTHOR

JANET HAMILL is the author of five books of poetry, prose poetry and short fiction. Her work had been nominated for the Pushcart Prize and the Poetry Society of America's William Carlos Williams Prize. *Tales from the Eternal Café* is her first complete collection of stories. In addition to her books, Janet has released two spoken word CD's with the band Lost Ceilings (previously Moving Star), featuring cameos by Lenny Kaye, Patti Smith, David Amram and Bob Holman. After three decades in New York City, Janet now resides in the Hudson Valley.

# Books on Three Rooms Press

## PHOTOGRAPHY-MEMOIR

Mike Watt
*On & Off Bass*

## FICTION

Michael T. Fournier
*Hidden Wheel*

Janet Hamill
*Tales from the Eternal Café*

Eamon Loingsigh
*Light of the Diddicoy*

Richard Vetere
*The Writers Afterlife*

## DADA

*Maintenant: Journal of
Contemporary Dada Art & Literature
(Annual poetry/art journal, since 2003)*

## SHORT STORY ANTHOLOGY

*Have a NYC: New York Short Stories*
Annual Short Fiction Anthology

## HUMOR

Peter Carlaftes
*A Year on Facebook*

## PLAYS

Madeline Artenberg &
Karen Hildebrand
*The Old In-and-Out*

Peter Carlaftes
*Triumph For Rent (3 Plays)*
*Teatrophy (3 More Plays)*

## TRANSLATIONS

Patrizia Gattaceca
*Isula d'Anima / Soul Island*
(poems by the author in Corsican with
English translations)

George Wallace
*EOS: Abductor of Men*
(poems by the author in English
with Greek translations)

Gerard Malanga
*Malanga Chasing Vallejo*
(new English translations of
selected poems of Cesar Vallejo,
with additional notes and photos)

## POETRY COLLECTIONS

Hala Alyan
*Atrium*

Peter Carlaftes
*DrunkYard Dog*
*I Fold with the Hand I Was Dealt*

Joie Cook
*When Night Salutes the Dawn*

Thomas Fucaloro
*It Starts from the Belly
  and Blooms*
*Inheriting Craziness is Like
  a Soft Halo of Light*

Patrizia Gattaceca
*Isula d'Anima / Soul Island*

Kat Georges
*Our Lady of the Hunger*
*Punk Rock Journal*

Robert Gibbons
*Close to the Tree*

Karen Hildebrand
*One Foot Out the Door*
*Take a Shot at Love*

Matthew Hupert
*Ism is a Retrovirus*

David Lawton
*Sharp Blue Stream*

Jane LeCroy
*Signature Play*

Dominique Lowell
*Sit Yr Ass Down or You Ain't gettin
  no Burger King*

Jane Ormerod
*Recreational Vehicles on Fire*
*Welcome to the Museum of Cattle*

Lisa Panepinto
*On This Borrowed Bike*

Angelo Verga
*Praise for What Remains*

George Wallace
*Poppin' Johnny*
*EOS: Abductor of Men*

# Three Rooms Press | New York, NY

Current Catalog: www.threeroomspress.com
Three Rooms Press Is Distributed by PGW